DEAD ENDINGS
Henry Ben Edom

Published by Swann + Bedlam

Copyright © 2024 by Henry Ben Edom and Swann +Bedlam

All rights reserved.

No part of this publication may be reproduced, distributed, or transmitted in any form or by any means, including photocopying, recording, or other electronic or mechanical methods, without the prior written permission of the publisher, except as permitted by U.S. copyright law. For permission requests, contact Swann + Bedlam.

The story, all names, characters, and incidents portrayed in this production are fictitious. No identification with actual persons (living or deceased), places, buildings, and products is intended or should be inferred.

Book Cover by Rotten Fantom

Formatting by Swann + Bedlam
Edited with blood, sweat, and tears by Swann + Bedlam
Graphic Logo by Rotten Fantom

Swann + Bedlam
an imprint of Punk AF Publishing
287 Exhibition St,
Melbourne, VIC 3000
Australia

swannbedlam.com

1st edition 2024

Leave A Review!!

By reading this book you are showing your support for indie authors and small presses like us. For this, we want to say thank you! If you would take a moment to leave a review whether it's on Amazon, Goodreads, or any other social media platform, we would very much appreciate it.

Books don't make themselves. Many countless hours go into creating the work you are about to read. Often times, indie authors you enjoy create these books as a result of raw passion, artistic expression, and pure drive, while also working day jobs. A review is a great tool to help get their books into as many hands as possible plus earn a piece of recognition for writers who truly deserve to have their names read and remembered.

At Swann + Bedlam we began publishing as a way to get wicked awesome books to readers like you. Our mission is to publish the offbeat, the macabre, the problem child, the outcast, and the flat-out weird. No genres, no boundaries, no agenda.

Once again thank you for reading and reviewing this work.

DON'T LET The maN bRING yOU dOWN.
Power to the people!

These are stories of necromancy.
Stories of us relating to our dead.
This one is for Väinö and Lalli.

LUSTMORD

The raven circled the barren tree tops like a black rag against the sky. It cried once and its friend replied from a distant mountain.

Micah slammed his shovel into the soil with both hands, penetrating a layer of bruised leaves. After a while his shovel hit something hard. The breeze chilled the sweat on his brow. He crouched and began removing the soil with cupped hands.

The brownish dome was unearthed first, then the sockets.

"Hello," whispered Micah.

He traced the shape of the skull with his fingers. He dug underneath, freed it from the ground and raised it to his face. A warm tingle ran below his navel. The skull had once had a pretty face on it. It had carried her soul. Her petite nose had covered the tear-drop hollows of the nostrils. Her lips had hidden the teeth, now earth-cracked and rugged.

Keeping the skull in one hand, he pulled a creased Polaroid from his pocket. A warm bulge throbbed in his jeans.

She came out from the dirty folds of the photo.

Micah set the skull on the ground. His eyes focused on the photo. Her pallid shape beside the tree. Her face contorted in a frozen scream. Her breasts resting against her stomach, thighs askew, unveiling a bloody bush.

Micah placed his thumb on the image of her severed arm. He opened his fly. The zipper's teeth caught his pubic hairs and bit some off. Cold wind licked the tip of his erection. He began to pound his clenched hand back and forth. He felt like he was in free fall. His penis had been growing lately; it seemed to enlarge each time he and Mama took another girl.

with every girl he and Mama had taken.

His muscles spasmed. He closed his eyes as his hand pumped in rapid fire. The free fall came to its end, and almost hurt.

Gasping, Micah looked down. The skull was now coated with sticky strands. His hand and the tip of his organ glistened.

He tucked himself back into his pants, wiped his hand on his trousers, and looked around. The burning urge remained inside him, even stronger now. He crouched closer to the skull and peered at the mess he had made. A raven cawed from above as if it knew what was going on, why he suddenly felt so different.

***

The camper was parked behind a hill on an

old logger road. Micah returned to the vehicle and placed the skull carefully on the passenger seat. He looked down the aisle and into the back of the camper where the coffin lay. Rasping sounds came from within it. Mama had been growing restless these last few days, awakening before sundown. This night she came out early.

Micah was seated by the table picking mud from under his fingernails with a hunting knife when she emerged. When he saw the wooden hatch being pushed up he sealed the covers on the window behind him, cutting off the blood-red sunset. The interior turned dark.

One of Mama's milky legs stretched out of the coffin. Her skin shone in the gloom. She grasped the sides of the coffin, and the vessel became like a dark maw spitting out the rest of her. She sat naked on the edge, her eyes hidden by raven hair impossible to delineate from the dark. Her lips opened in dry silence. She strode over to Micah.

Micah rested his knife on the table. Mama sniffed the air and glanced into the front of the vehicle. Her eyes rested on the skull on the passenger seat. Micah patted the pocket of his jacket for the reassuring feeling of the Polaroid hidden inside. He felt as if invisible hands had wrapped around his throat. He swallowed, trying to dispel the sensation.

Mama leaned toward him. Her blue-veined breasts dangled in his face. She grabbed his hair and yanked his head sideways. Micah screamed. Mama eased her grip, but didn't let go. She forced his mouth onto her tit. Micah hesitated, then started to suck.

"My little boy," said Mama.

Micah pressed closer and suckled like a hungry puppy.

Mama played with his hair tenderly now. "They want to hurt us. All of them. Unless you want us to die, you gotta understand."

Micah let the warm milk gather in his mouth before swallowing. A sense of comfort washed over him as he savored the final drops.

Mama clicked her tongue and brushed Micah's head with her palm. "My little ghoul," she whispered. "Are you ready to leave?"

Micah nodded. He wiped his mouth on his moth-eaten sleeve, tasting dust.

Mama walked into the front cabin and removed the covers from the windshield. Pale moonlight fell on her skin. Micah sat behind the wheel and reached for the keys, but Mama grasped his wrist before he could turn over the engine.

"I am starving," she said. "Feed me first."

Micah went to the kitchenette and took a

white metallic box from a cabinet. The box clanged against the burner as he set it down. The hinges creaked as he opened it. There were only a handful of syringes left, shiny in their plastic wrapping.

"We're almost out of them," he said.

Micah tore a syringe from its wrapping and pulled the plastic cap off the needle. Mama watched him expectantly from the cabin, licking her cracked lips and scratching her sides. "Can't go on like this. I'm starving, getting weaker."

Micah approached with the syringe between his teeth and a rubber tourniquet around his arm. He squeezed his fingers into a fist to pop his veins.

The sight of the syringe made Mama smile. Micah sat next to her with his bare arm braced atop his knee. He positioned the needle above a bulging vein, and prepared himself for a sensation of pain he'd never grown accustomed to.

Mama grasped his wrist. "Please, let me."

He gave her the syringe. A chill ran down his back. He gazed at the moon's pitted skin and began to drift away, until a sting pulled him back into the moment.

Mama shivered at the sight of his blood steadily filling the chamber. Once it was full she pulled the needle out. A single drop escaped and ran down his forearm. Mama leaned in and ran her tongue across his arm to lick the rivulet up.

"Never let anything go to waste," she said.

Mama always did as she taught. Theirs was the life of the ravens. Everything had its use.

She squirted the blood into her mouth as if taking a shot of liquor. Micah ignited the motor and waited for directions. The headlights came on and joined the glow of the moonbeams on the bleak woods.

"You remember the cabins from two winters ago?" Mama asked.

Micah nodded.

"Let's pay a visit to that couple who passed us the other night," Mama said. "I'm tired of these worn whores." She tossed the skull off the passenger seat. Micah watched it roll down the aisle and come to rest against Mama's coffin, which still loomed open, like a dark maw ready to devour.

"You'll get enough bones of your own one day," said Mama. "Enough to build a house!"

She tickled his ribs with a spider-like hand, then withdrew to the back of the camper to leaf through her photo album. Micah slid the polaroid from his pocket for a peek at the dead girl's tits. His pants grew tighter as his penis stiffened. He tucked the photo away and gripped the wheel. The silhouette of a raven crossed the moon's gaunt face. Two more followed, winging their way towards the mountains.

***

Mike slammed his hand on the screaming digital clock beside the bed. The alarm died and the blazing red digits blacked out for a moment. He yawned and pulled the blanket back over his chest. Lily rolled over beside him and packed herself against his side.

Mike looked up at the log-built ceiling and smelled the fresh wilderness beyond the cabin.

"Good to be out of the city," he said.

His last word became a yawn. He stretched, muscles still tight from two days spent hunched behind the wheel. But while his body felt stiff, his mind felt anything but. Hours of watching cities and roads stream by his window had cut his head loose from torturous schedules and the burden of managing his mother's affairs. He hadn't slept this easy in months.

Lily blinked in the morning light and ran her fingers down his chest. "It's the change alone," she said, as though she'd been reading his mind. "Sometimes we need a change to see what's important."

"Which is?" He asked.

"This." She snuggled her face into his neck

and slid her silken leg over his until she was pressing down on top of him. "Here and now."

"I kinda like where this is heading." Mike caressed her hips. Lily kissed him and yanked his underwear down.

During their drive to the cabin, Mike had wondered whether this was really the right time to pop the question. It was such a stressful period in their lives. He kept fidgeting with the ring in his pocket, as if he were afraid it would vanish into thin air, just like their relationship might. There were a thousand possible reasons things could go south. And yet, even after four years together, he and Lily were alright. Better than alright. Lily was the best thing that had ever happened to him. The best thing that kept happening to him, over and over again.

Presently he decided: tonight was the night. Lily was the one for him, right here, right now. Holding out for perfection would only make him lose what he already had.

***

Mike stopped to drink from his canteen and take in the sight of the woods. In the sun's dying light the lake below glimmered like a golden abyss.

"It's funny, the way the mind works," he said.

"What do you mean?" said Lily.

"Remember that woman we saw, on our way here through the woods? Well, for a second, when I saw her, I had this sharp, sinking feeling, like something had happened - something with Mom. And I thought, what if that's her ghost, appearing to me?"

Lily took his hand in hers. "Mike, you gotta stop blaming yourself. Stop worrying. Things just happen, that's life."

Mike let her words sink in and felt some of the stress drain away.

She leaned her head against his shoulder. "Whatever happens, you've taken good care of her, just like you've taken good care of me."

"I take good care of you, huh? Like this morning?" He gave Lily's bottom a pinch.

She laughed and folded her arms around him. "Let me guess, you're gonna take care of me tonight, too?"

He gave her nose a soft bite. "As these mountains are my witness."

"Okay, soldier. Lead me home." Despite her words she led him down a steep trail which provided the quickest route back to the cabin. Aware he was watching her, she jiggled her butt and received a welcome slap in response.

By the time they got back dusk had settled upon the still lake, and only the golden shards of the mountainside remained of the passing day. Lily bypassed the cabin and walked straight to the dock at the edge of the lake. She stripped off, adding her naked form to the landscape.

"Wanna join me?" she said.

"Sure." He nodded towards the dark cabin. "I'll just go get our towels and put the lights on."

"That stuff can wait. Come on!"

She ran up the creaking steps onto the jetty. Mike turned and headed towards the cabin nonetheless. He had something that couldn't wait. His fingers were aching to get hold of the engagement ring. Lily was right - he worried too much. But it was time to stop worrying, and start living.

He heard a splash behind him as Lily dove headfirst into the water, but he didn't turn. Instead he quickened his pace toward the cabin in the mountain's long shadow.

Lily resurfaced and looked at the rugged woods sloping from the mountain to the edge of the lake. From the water level everything was radiant with the blue of evening. Banks of mist hung over the water. The wet hair covering her ears muffled everything, but she could still make out the sound of her name being called behind her.

"Lily!"

She turned toward the dock, where Mike was crouched, waving her over with frantic movements. His expression was hard to make out in the dim light, but there was something about it which made her unsettled. She swam toward him, his beckoning hand saying faster, faster! She reached the dock and brushed her wet hair from her ears to hear him clearly.

"There's a boy," he said, as Lily began to pull herself out of the water.

"What do you mean, a boy?"

"In the cabin. Come up, now." Mike helped her onto the dock, then turned, as if sensing something she couldn't see.

An explosion ripped the night apart. Lily flinched. Her ears hissed in the aftermath.

Mike twitched and fell backward, striking his skull against the dock beside her feet.

Lily saw - a boy? - at the base of the dock, his face shaded by a hooded raincoat. He aimed a handgun at Mike, even though Mike was already on the ground, so still, his expression frozen, his eyes open on a living nightmare from which he would never awake.

***

The woman stood handcuffed to a stout wooden pillar in the center of the cabin. Her tear-streaked features shone beneath a dirty light bulb which cast deep shadows under her chin and breasts. Micah circled around her, watching her through the Polaroid camera.

"What are you doing?" she gasped.

The question compelled Micah to lower the camera. For a moment his naked eyes met hers. Then he raised the Polaroid back to his face and zoomed in on her breasts by slowly stepping closer.

"Why?" she asked.

Micah said nothing. Heat flushed his face.

"Why'd you do that to him?" she asked.

Micah remained silent and peered at her through the Polaroid, moving his gaze up and down her body. Every detail of her skin burned his insides, inviting him to touch her - but he didn't. He wanted to photograph her, to collect every detail of her - but he couldn't. He'd run out of film if he started shooting before Mama arrived. But perhaps just one -

He snapped a single image of her crying face. Her grief made it impossible for him to memorialize her beauty in any other way.

All at once a sense of disquiet rose up in Micah, stemming from a feeling he couldn't - wouldn't - bring himself to articulate. He fled from the cabin. Her scream followed him, then died behind the wall.

"She's gorgeous."

The sound of Mama's voice shrank Micah's heart. She walked from darkness into moonlight, her ribcage drawn with stark shadows on her sides. Soil rustled as she dragged her favorite scythe alongside her, its blade plowing a furrow in her wake.

"The male?" she asked.

Micah fidgeted with the camera hanging by a strap from his neck.

"Dead," he said. "Shot him."

He placed a finger on his chest to mark the spot where he'd shot the man, though he couldn't be sure of the exact location of the wound. The moment of the shooting was hazy, now that he tried to recall it. A foggy stretch until the details of the woman's body were seen through the camera. He felt distant from himself. Strange and unfit inside his chest.

Mama hefted the blade onto her shoulder, holding it with both hands like she was about to hit a baseball. Micah placed his finger on the Polaroid's trigger, but almost couldn't feel it. He followed Mama into the cabin and raised the viewfinder to his eye.

The woman was struggling to escape her

bonds. With a flash Micah caught the terrified first contact between her and Mama. The camera buzzed and spat the photograph on the floor.

The camera flashed again as Mama's blade came down and sliced so deep it almost cut the woman's left arm off.

Blood gushed. The woman screamed. A third flash found her struggling so hard against her bonds the strip of flesh connecting her wounded arm to her trunk began to rip.

Mama hefted the blade and took a swing at the woman's uninjured side. Her right arm came off just below the shoulder and fell to the floor in a shower of red. Mama's blade bit deep into the pillar and stuck there.

Micah took the woman's picture again. Agony had twisted her features; she barely looked human anymore. She let out an animal scream and fled towards the cabin door. Her severed arm trailed after her, still handcuffed to the other.

"Get her!" Mama screamed as she tried to wrench her blade from the pillar.

Micah dropped the Polaroid and let it dangle from the neck strap as he gave chase. He was halfway across the room when he slipped on the blood-splattered floor and fell to one knee. As he went down he reached out and grabbed the woman's severed arm as it trailed after her like a pet on a leash. The woman didn't stop, not even when the slack on the handcuff chain ran out.

For a moment the strip of flesh tethering her half-severed arm to her trunk grew taut; then it stretched and snapped like cheap leather. Micah found himself holding a pair of severed arms bound by handcuffs. He watched as the woman, still running, tore through the doorway and into the darkness beyond.

Micah leapt up and followed the woman outside. She wasn't screaming anymore. She lay face-down and motionless with blood gushing from her stumps. Micah straddled her legs; his hands slid across her bloody skin as he turned her onto her back. Mama emerged from the cabin with her blade hoisted; her shadow fell upon them like an image of the reaper descending.

The woman was still alive, but barely. Her wide eyes stared up at Micah. He looked away and realized his hands were on her breasts. The woman twitched. Whether she sought to welcome death or somehow escape it, Micah didn't know. He only grasped tighter, feeling her hard nipples against his palms.

Intense heat surged into his crotch. He moaned as his pants filled with stickiness. He sank into a fetal position beside the woman, who stared into his eyes. Her body moved, not because she willed it to, but because Mama's blade was in her belly, carving her deep enough to feed the earth with her entrails. Micah's bliss turned to sickness. For a moment he hoped the woman would wake. The northern wind blew across his face, indifferent to who it licked.

Ravens cawed in dark canopies, keeping their distance; they knew not to disturb Mama's work. Layer by layer the woman was opened like a piece of fruit, her insides steaming in the cold air. Mama worked with bare hands, with care, handling the woman's intestines like poisonous snakes she didn't want to irritate. Going deeper into the black, yellowish white and red, opening wider the leaves of flesh, she teased the woman open, dug, pulled, and gouged, until she knelt in a dark, red mountain of insides made outsides. Finally, using the handle of her scythe like a maul, Mama cracked the woman's ribs, pulled them apart, and reached inside. When she rose she held out the woman's most precious organ for the moon to admire.

Micah let the camera's flash strike against the scene.

Mama looked directly into the camera and ate the woman's heart in a single mouthful. It crawled down her throat and vanished, like a mouth down the gullet of a snake.

Micah took one last photograph, eternalizing her in her prime.

***

Micah awoke in his bunk. It was daylight outside, and pinpricks of sunlight shone through the covers on the windows. He forced himself up. The black leather jacket he'd found in the couple's car lay at his feet. Its silver buttons and zippers glinted in the light as he shrugged it on. His hands emerged from the sleeves only barely. He put them in his pockets and took a few turns. The leather creaked as he slicked his hair back with his palms. If only he had a pair of dark sunglasses like the ones he'd seen on that film poster.

The whole of the previous night felt hazy, like a distant memory.

Micah felt the corner of the photo album against his toe. It lay on the floor, where it had been hidden by the jacket. He picked it up and placed it on the table. The binding opened with a dry crunch.

Micah flipped through heavy cardboard pages covered with glued-on photographs, newspaper articles, and black markings drawn by Mama. He couldn't read, but he knew the curvy signs - the numbers - which Mama had drawn on the pages signified the passage of time, like autumn following summer.

He peered at faces that didn't exist anymore, consumed in one way or another, either by Mama or by the rot. Faces lacerated, bruised into purple and black swollen messes. Then there were faces he'd never seen in the flesh, gritty black-and-white photos of a little baby, sometimes with adults, sometimes alone.

Micah turned the sheets until he arrived at the last page, where the latest photos lay in disarray inside a plastic pocket. He removed them and spread some out upon the page. The woman from the previous night stared at him again, her eyes red from the flash.

The same inexpressible unease Micah had felt in the cabin rolled through him again, even worse this time. With the sense of horror came spikes of pain radiating through his chest. Feeling like he was choking, he turned the photo over. Slowly the strange feeling stopped skinning him alive. He released himself from the heavy jacket and felt a partial ease fall upon his shoulders. He closed the album, and was about to set it back on the floor, when he spotted a little black box resting nearby. Leaving the album on the table, he picked up the black box and wiped the dust from its soft fabric coating. He'd never seen the box before;

it must have spilled out from one of the jacket's many pockets. He popped the lid and saw a row of diamonds glittering like royal teeth.

Micah glanced at Mama's coffin, then back at the ring. It must have been meant for the woman from the photo, to signify that way in which two people stay together forever. He closed the box and zipped it away inside the jacket's chest pocket.

***

In the back of her family's sedan, Jessica scratched her arm, which itched as if bugs were crawling under the skin. Luckily she was too high to be worried that much.

Her Mom sat in the front passenger seat; her middle-aged flesh, cloaked in an unflattering dress, spilled over the central console. Dad stood outside with a cigarette burning in his hand. Its smoke crept through the open driver's side window in ethereal waves.

A white plastic bag sat beside Jessica like a meteor none of them wanted to believe had hit them. But it had. The way the nurse had bundled Billy's little, bloody clothes into it had made Mom scream until she'd almost passed out. Afterwards she was quiet, like a frozen lake, nodding along with whatever the doctor said, though it was clear she understood none of it.

But Jessica understood.

Billy was dead.

Her little brother had passed away in an accident that was nothing but a careless mistake. That stupid boy should have watched where he was running. Jessica should have watched where he was going. Now that scream of warning, which had come out too late, somehow still rolled around inside her, like lightning refusing to strike.

Luckily today she was high enough not to feel a thing.

Mom stopped fidgeting with her dress. Her head bobbed as if she were listening to music no one else could hear. Then she grew still, and a wail of grief erupted from her mouth like sound through a speaker. It seemed to go on and on. Dad turned toward the fast food restaurant across the hospital parking lot, and lit another smoke.

Jessica stared at the back of her mother's head and began to count stray hairs caught in a sunbeam. One, two, three, four...the seemingly infinite chain progressed, accompanied by the haunting realization that she really shouldn't have left Billy alone at that moment.

***

Jessica kept herself high well past the funeral and stayed in her room whenever she wasn't particularly needed, which was pretty much always. She scored drugs by giving blowjobs to dealers. She didn't need heavy weight; she wasn't a junkie. Just a high school bitch with big tits, they said.

'Daddy's angel.'

The dealer who called her that had no idea how close he'd come to having his dick bitten off. But Jessica sucked it instead, keeping herself supplied for a few more days.

She was a ghost inside the house, and wished to remain so as much as possible. She kept her skull nice and empty with whatever she could get with her lips. Those filthy lips, which she kept sparkling with continuous applications of balms and glosses. So far she'd done almost everything a person could smoke, eat, or snort; all that remained was to inject, and she'd begun to dream of shooting herself up ever since Mom had decided to use her small daily allotment of words to blame her for Billy's death.

She'd heard of the oblivion it offered. And she needed oblivion somehow. She couldn't find it in orgasm; after all those dealer dicks she couldn't dream of normal sex like her friends, all of whom had more or less fled from the black gloom around her. She dreamed of a sharp and deep penetration - the sharpest, the deepest - something to spray her into nothingness, a form of outrageous ecstasy so loud it would drown her out and leave her body walking around like a living dead thing. Such a fire exit out of existence sounded almost too good to be true.

Presently Jessica heard Dad's steps heading down the hall toward her room. The sound stopped, and she knew he had paused outside Billy's old room. She opened the window to flush out the smoke from her almost-finished joint, then dropped the joint itself into a jar of dirty water hidden between the wall and her bed.

Dad resumed his approach and knocked on her door.

"Yeah?" she said.

The door opened. From the look on Dad's face it was clear he could smell what Jessica had been smoking.

"I'd like you to come downstairs," he said.

"Why?" she asked.

"Please."

He walked away, leaving the door open. Jessica followed him downstairs and found the front door open. Mom was on the threshold, dressed only in her nightgown, staring at the road. In such a state, how could she ever question Jessica's coping skills? The woman was a miserable wreck.

Dad beckoned them out into the bright front yard. His face had a strange, vibrant sparkle to it. Jessica joined him in the sunlight. He pointed to a huge, pristine white motor home parked outside the house.

"We're leaving," he said.

"What?"

Jessica looked to Mom, but the woman just stared at the giant RV with empty eyes.

"It's ours," said Dad. He stared at the motor home as if unable to take his eyes off it. "A new beginning."

Jessica almost laughed. "For fucks sake," was all she managed to say.

***

While the disappearance of Mike Georges and Lily Paxton, a couple from Fort Collins, Colorado, remains unsolved, the state police, assisted by volunteer groups, have expanded their search deeper into the wilderness surrounding...

Mama sat on the foot of the bed and blocked Micah's view of Lily's smiling face on the TV. Micah craned his head to look past her, but Lily's face was already gone, replaced by images of patrol cars parked along a woodland road. The image switched to an old woman being interviewed while text scrolled across the bottom of the screen.

Mama walked to the TV and turned it off with a shaky finger. She hadn't eaten anything while they'd stayed in this motel. She walked to the window and pulled the blind back just a fraction to peer outside. The room shook as a truck barreled down the road running past the motel toward the highway.

During the past few weeks, Micah had visited a few shops and gas stations in the daytime. He'd bought himself a pair of sunglasses like the ones from that movie poster. They'd been at the motel for a few nights, and Micah was enjoying hot baths and TV. But Mama was growing restless again. She slept the whole day in her pine box, coming into the hotel room just before dark.

"It hurts," said Mama. "Those photos you keep stealing from me." As she returned to the bed she swiped at Micah's leather jacket, which hung from a hook on the wall.

Micah's cheeks grew hot. He turned his gaze toward his hands, which Mama cupped inside hers. Gently she circled his knuckles with her thumbs as though she were counting them. Micah didn't know what to say. His throat felt swollen, as if a fistful of sand had been forced inside of it.

"I just want to make you happy." Mama

stripped off her shirt and caressed her swollen breasts. "Please."

Micah lay his head on her lap and took a nipple in his mouth. He couldn't stop thinking about Lily's breasts, a photo of which he had hidden in the inner pocket of his jacket. He'd masturbated over it twice while Mama had slept, and had shot loads of sticky liquid on the bathroom tile.

He stared at his jacket while suckling on Mama's tit, thinking of the hidden photo and how many loads Mike must have shot into Lily while the two of them were still alive. He would have been able to look her in the face while he came, unlike Micah, who'd had to cut her face from the Polaroids because of how horrible she'd looked when she was dying.

His stomach now full, he kept his head on Mama's lap while she pulled her shirt back on. Mama smiled and ran her fingers through his hair.

"How about we look at them together?" she asked.

Micah nodded, but he knew Mama wasn't ready to look at the photos yet; she had something else on her mind. She leaned closer and brushed the tip of her nose against his in a circular motion.

"It's been a while," she said.

Without saying a word, Micah fetched the syringe box and got back on the bed to make the preparations. He tied on the tourniquet, pumped his fist, and aimed the pipette at his juiciest vein. As he was about to plunge the needle in, Mama rocked back and forth restlessly, shaking the bed, spoiling his aim.

"Please!" Micah said as he struggled to hold the needle steady.

But Mama didn't stop rocking. Her eyes flitted between his face and his bulging veins. He hadn't seen her this hungry in a long time. "Could you..."

"Could I what?" said Micah.

"Could you use the razor instead?"

Once again without a word, Micah returned to the box and picked his way past sealed syringes and needles until he found the surgical blade at the bottom of the kit. He placed it on the bed. It felt light in its wrappings, its plastic handle heavier than its gentle, shining blade.

He unwrapped the blade and straightened his arm to expose the soft flesh. The blade sliced with burning precision, parting skin from skin as though opening an envelope. The first fiery sting transformed into a dull ache and blood welled up on the lips of the wound.

Mama craned her head toward him. Micah brought the wound to her mouth. She began to suck, her tongue exploring the lacerated tissue. Micah clenched his teeth; this was worse than the needle. Carried away by her bloodlust, Mama gnawed at the flesh around the incision, creating fresh lacerations to suck on.

Micah tried to imagine something else, tried to imagine Lily with him on the bed, gasping, shaking the mattress, but every time he conjured her image in his mind her skin erupted with bleeding furrows and her guts spilled out from the hollow of her stomach, forcing him to stop and start the fantasy over again. Again and again he tried to picture her whole and unsullied, until he felt exhausted from fighting to hold her imaginary body together.

Finally Mama finished, rolled onto her stomach, and opened the photo album lying beside them. Micah went to the bathroom and pressed a thick wad of toilet paper against the wound. He couldn't tell which hurt worse - the skin bitten raw or the initial cut. When the bleeding abated he left the bathroom and lay on the bed by Mama's side.

Mama flicked the pages back and forth a few times, then settled on a page with a photo of herself biting a young girl's neck from behind. Micah couldn't remember the girl at all.

"Would you ever believe she wanted it?" Mama traced the girl's contorted face with her finger, almost as if she wanted to brush her hair. "And

I almost hesitated." She laughed. "You know what cats do to their sick kittens? The ones too weak to survive?"

Micah shook his head. The throbbing in his arm had lessened to a dull ache smoldering under the compress of toilet tissue. He could feel a migraine coming on.

"They love them too much to abandon them to die alone," Mama continued. "So they eat them. They never leave someone weak to grow up alone. It keeps them together forever. Out there," Mama nodded towards the sealed windows, "it's nothing but loneliness and cruelty. Loneliness..." She turned the page, revealing a photo of a girl whose severed head sat atop her own torso and seemed to be gazing up at the sky. "...and cruelty. But the funny thing is, sometimes the mother eats the kittens anyway, even the strong and healthy ones."

"Why?" Micah asked.

Mama smiled. "Love is hard to explain."

Micah looked at the dried bloodstains on the photos. Now his head felt like it was in a vice. He knew he'd shot all these photos; he should have been used to the sight of them, but right now they made him feel like he was choking. The unease was upon him again, nameless and unnameable, clashing with his lust. A part of him wanted to go and masturbate to the image of the naked torso in that last picture, but he could only imagine his own hand falling off, unraveling from where he had cut his arm. His stomach churned as though worms were roasting inside it and needed to be puked up. He closed his eyes tightly.

Micah?

He heard Mama's voice from somewhere beyond far away. He tried to answer, but she was so very distant.

Something or someone shook him. Either into oblivion or out of it. The difference was incomprehensible. His mouth tasted only blood.

...Micah...?

***

Jessica sat on a creamy faux-leather sofa beside the motor home's kitchenette. In the front cabin Dad whistled something too broken to be a melody.

The vehicle's eight wheels did their best to smooth out the bumps on the road, but Jessica felt sick nevertheless. She slid the window ajar and rested her head against the pane. Dad had steered them once again onto some rugged detour, and the road was but a scar in a wooded landscape somewhere between the big highways. As to exactly where they were going, Jessica had no clue. 'North' was the answer she'd been given. 'Perhaps Canada. Maybe until Alaska.' In reality she knew Dad had no idea. He just wanted to drive, and Mom didn't care. Not about the destination, not about anything. She stared through everything with dead indifference, and seemed to have aged two decades over the past two weeks. The only time Mom had shown any emotion during the trip was when Jessica had placed her bag on the sleeping compartment's empty fourth bunk. Mom had screamed that it wasn't Jessica's bed. Afterwards she had regained her diminished senses and resumed her silence.

Presently the setting sun hung a loose golden wreath over the landscape, deepening every shadow. Was Jessica the only one sane enough to just want to talk about Billy? The only one brave enough to admit she felt utterly sick? She glanced into the sleeping compartment, where Mom lay on her berth, staring at the bottom of the upper bunk, her head bouncing from every bump on the road. Jessica was almost happy Billy wasn't here to see how badly they were doing.

The brakes screamed and the RV came to a stop. Jessica was yanked away from the window and slammed back against it.

"What the fuck!"

Jessica stood up, trembling. Mom had fallen to the floor, but still wore the same stupefied expression on her face. Jessica turned towards the front cabin.

"Dad?" She called. "Dad!"

Dad slowly rose up from behind the wheel.

"I...I guess I fell asleep. S-sorry."

"Are you okay?"

"Yeah, I'm alright." He rubbed his eyes, then peered into the sleeping compartment, where Mom had already crawled back into her bunk to resume her vacant staring.

Jessica looked at her shaking hands. "We can't go on like this. Fuck!" She opened the side door and ran out into the wind.

Dad followed her outside and began to inspect the vehicle. "It must have been just a bump in the road," he said, staring at the fishtailing tire marks he'd left on the blacktop. "Didn't hit anything."

"You've been driving for what, sixteen hours?" said Jessica. "You gotta sleep."

Dad looked at the darkening sky. "Guess you're right." He headed back towards the RV with drooping shoulders.

Jessica followed. "Hey, Dad. It's okay. Shit happens, yeah?"

Dad glanced back at her as if he were about to say something, but only nodded and climbed back into the van.

Now alone, Jessica listened to the wind whistle through the crimson forest. Her heart still raced. She reached into her pocket and caressed the joints in her cigarette pack. Slowly she wandered away from the van, following the road. Soon the RV was a dim shape behind her, stark and black in the sunset, like a fallen obelisk. Then a trail mouth opened up to invite her into the woods for a few solitary moments.

***

Micah opened his eyes. He lay somewhere dark, on his side, one arm trapped senseless beneath him while a wooden lid pressed against him from above. The air stank of rot.

He was inside the coffin.

Mama's coffin.

He shifted his weight and realized there was something lying across his waist, something long and slender, like a tree branch, or...

Whatever it was slipped off him, slid down his stomach, and hit the bottom of the box with a metallic clank. He felt the object with his fingers. It was soft and fleshy, tapering, with something hard and cold around it. It was one of Lily's arms, still handcuffed to the other. Mama had kept them in the box this whole time.

Micah coughed and took a breath of air dense with decay. A hand reached around him and grabbed his wrist.

"Are you awake?" Mama whispered into his ear.

Micah nodded.

Mama placed a cold hand upon his forehead. "How are you feeling?"

"Hot. Everything hurts." He tried to wriggle away from the severed arms; the stench of them seemed to grow by the second.

"Rest now. You'll be alright." Mama cradled his head against her chest. "It's just a fever."

Micah tried to relax, but he couldn't sleep anymore. Mama had no trouble sleeping. Her breath brushed the back of his neck. Her sleeping sighs were like whispers he couldn't make sense of. He thought about cats eating their kittens. He tried to squirm away from her, but there was no room. The sense of confinement was almost overwhelming. In this tiny space permeated with stench even the darkness felt like a physical thing, a weighted blanket crushing him close to Mama.

Lily's arms were sandwiched between his crotch and the side of the box. Her fingers caressed him whenever he moved. He explored Lily's arms with his fingers. Shriveled joints, soft openings, strips of loose skin. Lustmord made him sick to his stomach, but he couldn't stop. As he wrapped the dead fingers around his member he felt like the loneliest person in the world, lonely in a way Mama could never understand.

***

Dad wiped sweat off his brow and left a black smudge in its place. He pointed his wrench at the front tire. "The axle's broken."

Jessica looked at the sunny road behind the RV. "We drove at least an hour."

Dad sighed. "Yeah, we did. I guess if we just keep going up the road…"

Jessica looked at the isolated road winding into the woods ahead of them. "Dad, there's nothing there."

"Gotta be something."

"That's the freaking reason why you brought us here, as if some miracle awaits us at the end of some country road? We either wait for help, or we walk back. The junction's not that far."

"45 minutes, driving," said Dad in a defeated tone.

Jessica did the math in her head. "Well, there might be some…I don't know, a farm or whatever on one of those side roads we passed along the way."

Dad thought about it, his gaze lost in the horizon. "You're right, I suppose. I'm sorry." He looked like a bullied kid in a school hallway. Before Billy's death Jessica had never thought about her parents that way. Lost. Wandering in the dark with no idea what to do with their lives.

"It's okay," said Jessica, "we're all in this."

Her comment must have taken him off guard. Tears began to flow down his cheeks. Without thinking, Jessica wrapped her arms around him and pressed her face into his shoulder. For a moment Dad clung to her as though he were the child.

"Hold on, dad. I need you too. Mom needs us."

Dad nodded. Slowly his quiet sobbing began to ease. He sniffed and spoke almost in a whisper. "How about...how about I take a walk down the road. You take care of Mom while I find some help, and we'll catch up in a few hours."

"Sounds like a plan," Jessica said.

He stroked her hair, then headed off back in the direction they had come from. Soon he vanished into the horizon.

Jessica went back to the RV and stopped at the doorway to look inside. A black cloth hung over Mom's bunk like a shroud.

"Mom?" she called. "Are you awake?"

No answer. The space between them felt like a bottleneck of sorrow that would crush her if she tried to cross it. She stayed in the warm sun and lit a smoke. It was going to be a long fucking day.

***

The old man came out of the house with a shotgun and stepped into the glare of the van's headlights. Micah closed his eyes in panic. In his mind's eye he saw his own head exploding as the man blasted him through the windshield. But the man was dazed by the glare of the lights, and Mama was fast. She came from the shadows like a ghost and blew out his kneecap with the handgun. He dropped the shotgun and went down. Then his chin met with the barrel of his own gun, and promptly ceased to be.

Micah sat in the car as Mama went inside. Slowly the vision of his own skull exploding stopped repeating in his head.

After a while Mama emerged from the house. Naked and bloody, she came to the van and motioned for him to bring the camera by raising her hands in front of her face as if she were holding an invisible box. Micah nodded and got out of the van with the Polaroid hanging from his neck by the strap.

The old porch groaned beneath his weight. The paint on the timbers was cracked like dry mud. The downstairs was a single large room serving as a kitchen, living room, and bedroom all in one. Beside the staircase was a wheelchair too small for the dead man. Micah began to get an idea of what Mama had been doing these past few hours he'd spent sitting in the car.

"This was a surprise," said Mama as she began to climb the staircase.

Micah followed her up carpeted stairs spattered with blood. Growing thicker on the landing, the blood trail led to a room with green walls. He glanced inside and saw a bed in the middle overflowing with red butchery.

"She didn't fight at all," said Mama as she sat on the bed. Wet intestines slithered over each other as the mattress sagged beneath her weight. Between the scattered remains were strips of a purple dress with flowers on it, which now appeared to be growing from a field of gore.

"Can you imagine that old man carrying her down the stairs every day and moving her with that wheelchair?" said Mama as she fingered the remains. "Eventually he would have died and left her here all alone."

Mama lay on her side and wallowed in the scarlet puzzle that had once been a girl. She touched her breasts with bloody hands. "Come onto the bed with me."

Micah hesitated, then went to her. The nameless abhorrence welled up inside and made his stomach churn as he touched the sheets and felt the girl's bits under his palms. He should have been used to this by now, and yet -

Vomit exploded from his mouth onto the bed beside Mama's legs.

"My little boy."

Mama brushed Micah's hair while he wiped his mouth on his sleeve. Bitterness lingered in his airways. He reached for Mama's breast and began to suck. Warm milk oozed into his mouth. As Micah drank, Mama ate the girl's heart, and he felt her chest expanding as the girl became part of her.

Her alone, he realized.

He looked up at Mama's bloody lips. There she was, somewhere inside.

Lily.

In a happy place with Mama. With all the other girls.

"Don't wanna rot apart," he whispered, his voice still rough from the vomiting.

He raised the camera and turned it toward himself. He stared into the black abyss of its eye and smiled.

Eat me too, he almost said, and pressed the trigger, imagining himself in Mama's photo album. The camera disgorged the photo onto the sheet.

Mama tensed and sat up. He sat up likewise and followed her gaze to the window. Outside was green pasture melting into an azure sky. For a moment it looked empty. Then Micah saw him too, a stranger walking down the road toward the house.

Mama's lip curled back in a sneer, showing canines etched in clotted red. "Get him," she hissed, the blacks of her eyes like reptilian tongues in the sun.

Micah's pulse pounded in his ears. He clutched the camera to his chest and tried to pick up the photograph, but it had disappeared into the gore.

Mama pushed him off the bed. "Forget the camera. Take the pistol and your knife."

Micah unslung the camera from his neck and gave it to her.

"That man will find the corpse soon," she said. "Hurry up."

Her tone made Micah shiver as he headed for the door. Suddenly the same blackness that had devoured his memory when he'd shot Mike was looming at the edge of his perception, ready to devour him again. But Micah didn't want it to. Not anymore. This would be his turn.

Mama's voice made him pause on the threshold. "Micah, make me proud. Make him suffer."

***

Micah watched the man come up the drive, his sullen eyes trained on the ground in front of him, his arms dangling at his sides like heavy rags. He showed no sign of being familiar with the house, nor any sign that he could sense anything was wrong - at least not yet.

Lurking in the shadows, Micah seized the moment. He crept to the front door and waited till the man's line of sight to the house was blocked by the van. Then he rushed into the light, passing the old man's corpse, its head like a whacked tomato drying in the sun. He reached behind his back and grasped the handle of the pistol, always cold as winter no matter the weather.

He stepped around the van and into the man's line of sight. The man stopped and stared as Micah pulled the pistol out. The spot Micah had chosen was perfect; not only was it an ideal point to ambush the visitor, but the presence of the van blocked Mama's view from the upstairs window.

The man stared at the barrel of the gun and

raised his arms like a saint in church.

"Don't, please," he said.

The pistol began to tremble in Micah's hand. He tightened his grip and aimed for center mass.

"I've got money," the man said, his eyes wide and frantic. He pulled a brown leather wallet from his pocket and threw it at Micah's feet, where it bounced and kicked up dust.

"I don't want any trouble, please."

Micah raised a finger to his lips to silence the man. There was grime on the finger and he licked it, tasting dirt and dried blood, the only taste he truly knew.

The man trembled and screwed his eyes shut, as if sensing the closeness of death.

The gun began to tremble in Micah's grip again. He grabbed it with both hands to stop it from shaking. He glanced down and saw little faces peeking out of the man's wallet, passport-sized photos of a smiling boy and a girl with dark eyes, her lips parted as if in a whisper.

The man opened his eyes and saw where Micah was looking.

"Let them be," he said. "Please!"

Realizing his aim had dropped off again, Micah pointed the pistol at the center of the man's chest for the third time.

In response, the man pressed his palms against his mouth the same way Mama did if her stomach could no longer hold a heart she had eaten. But the man didn't puke. He poured muffled prayers into his fingers as his horrified eyes moved between Micah and the photos.

Micah stepped closer and pressed the barrel of the pistol against the man's nose. Once again he pictured himself amongst the images in Mama's album.

"Kill me," Micah whispered.

The man stopped whimpering and stared at him. "What?"

Micah pressed the barrel of the pistol more firmly against the man's nose.

"Take the gun," he said. "Kill me."

The man drew back and stared at Micah. For a moment his eyes seemed to answer with a sweet and terrifying "yes." Then he shook his head. "No, you're just a child, I..."

Micah squeezed the trigger.

The man's dark eyes bloomed like two black suns as the bullet passed through his nose and came out the back of his head in a spray of blood and chunks. Micah's ears rang. The man fell facedown on Micah's foot and trembled in a mute death rattle.

Micah watched the blood puddle and seep

into the soil. Cold shivers ran through his body. He felt someone place a hand on his shoulder, and for a second he hoped it was someone new, someone who could do what the dead man had failed to do. Then a voice he knew well cut through the ringing in his ears and the echoing thunder of the gun.

"He's not alone," said Mama.

She stood behind him in the sunlight, all naked, the blood upon her like a second skin, red and cracking like the soil of the desert at dusk. She scraped her gore-encrusted fingernails down the back of his scalp as though inflicting a punishment for an unnamed crime.

"He said he had a family," said Mama. "And he came from over there."

Mama nodded towards the emptiness beyond the hills and sniffed the wind as though she could smell her prey. She knelt by the dead man.

"Soon they will be praying to join him. But first, there's one more thing to do."

***

Jessica walked Mom to the shower and helped wash off the reek of her immobility. Afterwards Mom smiled for a moment. Then she glanced at the empty fourth bunk, and lay back down without a word.

As crushing as the situation was, Jessica still had hope. There was still some faint thread of sense running through Mom's head. Enough sense to eat, have a shower, and realize Billy was dead and gone. In time, hopefully, that thread of sense would be enough to drag her out of this abyss and help her to cope.

Enough to help me cope, too, thought Jessica.

For now, they were all but zombies of grief. Ruins in human shape. If there was a God overseeing their journey through life, he liked to tend his flock with fire and iron.

***

Mama cut the man's head from the torso. The expression baked into the face was tired and miserable, as if some nightmare had entered the dead man and drowned his soul long before Micah had taken the shot.

Micah hadn't known the man, but he knew the sorrow in those eyes. It was closer to him than his own flesh.

Mama knelt by the leaking trunk of the body and continued her work. Micah watched the flesh of the abdomen part in the wake of her blade, slick reds and yellows unveiled in the cavity. She sliced across the chest below the ribs, ripping open a red mouth in the center of the torso. She reached into that mouth and tore out a clump of tight muscle and torn arteries.

"Here." She placed the heart in Micah's cupped hands.

It was wet and warm, as if it possessed some numinous power.

"Go ahead," said Mama.

Micah felt his gorge rise. His stomach screamed *No*.

"Eat," said Mama.

Micah bit into the heart. The tissue was viscous and tough. It resisted at first, then gave way beneath his teeth. Blood trickled into his mouth from a ruptured ventricle. He stuck his tongue inside and licked the chamber clean until he had to gasp for air.

Mama smiled and licked her own dripping hand until a patch of pale skin became visible amongst the coat of blood.

Micah took a desperate breath which transformed into a scream and sent the birds flying from nearby trees. He sank his fingers into the heart's jagged holes and pulled until the organ ripped in half.

Meanwhile the premature ghost of the moon appeared on the horizon, and the sun shed its yellow skin for crimson, giving out a colder caress as the day began to die.

"Isn't it beautiful?" said Mama. "What nature does with storms, cats with their fangs, and crows with their beaks, we do with knives. Death and the grave does this to us all. Mutilation is the only language all beings speak. Wounds are the entrances to every heart."

Micah felt the electric oppression of the hunt begin to gather in the air. From the roof of the death house - a home transformed into a crypt - the gathered ravens cawed, giving their blessing to the pain and death Micah and Mama were about to inflict.

A black storm rolled through Micah's mind. He looked at the body of the man whose blood caked his gums. He looked at his own flesh and felt tired of all the things it made him desire. He was tired of this black hole inside himself never being filled. The faces of all the girls whose photos he'd masturbated over swarmed into his mind. He heard them screaming a ghostly dirge. Nameless abhorrence enveloped him.

Without a word he headed for the death house. He entered the shadows and walked towards the stairs. A fat fly buzzed into the upstairs room. He followed it inside and sat on the bed.

The air was thick and dead. Micah found

the photograph he had taken beside a gaping hole in the girl's torso. He held it up and peered at his own smiling image. His heart raced.

He pulled down his pants and began to yank on his penis without restraint, but the organ refused to grow no matter how much he pulled and squeezed. All he felt was pain as he tortured his flesh with desperate tugging. A dull weight pressed against his chest as though an invisible slab were atop him.

The fly he had followed into the room circled the dead girl's eyeball. Micah yanked harder, but the itch of desire inside of him wouldn't move down to his crotch. It remained in his chest, imprisoned. The buzzing of the fly was like torture.

He gave up and let his limp organ rest between his legs. He felt nothing.

The fly alighted on the eyeball and buzzed.

Micah pulled out his knife in a reverse grip and stabbed it deep into the eye. The fly was no more. The dead girl seemed to smile at him. He yanked out the blade and drove it back down into the socket. The girl's mouth opened, and seemed to emit a silent laugh.

Micah yanked out the knife. He grasped her chin and twisted her face so that her remaining eye, cold and indifferent, seemed to stare straight at him.

He stabbed the eye over and over, ramming the blade deep into the skull, cracking bone, unleashing strange odors from within. He didn't stop until the socket was empty and black. Straddling the girl's chest he tore at her face, first with the blade, then with his fingers and nails, until her visage was nothing but a broken mess.

Panting, he turned from the carnage and looked at the Polaroid image of his own face. He looked at the blade dripping blood from the mutilated girl. He looked down at the penis which hung in limp shame beneath his belly.

A cold shiver ran down his spine as he pressed the edge of the blade against the base of his penis. One by one he tightened his fingers around the handle. He was just a single cut away from freeing himself from himself.

But the blare of the van's horn stopped him, cutting through the walls of the house like the call of some monstrous beast.

He lowered the knife and walked to the window. There was Mama in the van, blasting the horn, looking up at him through the windshield.

Micah pulled his pants up and cleaned his blade on one of the few clean sections of the bedsheet. He shivered as he descended the stairs, pulled down by the summons of the horn. He climbed into the van and slipped the photo of himself into the album with all the pictures of the girls. Then he slumped into the driver's seat. Mama sat beside him with the dead man's head on her lap. His arms, cleft from the torso but still connected by strips of skin and muscle, hung around her shoulders like a stole; the fingers of one hand clutched at her breast. She held his wallet open, speaking to the children in the photos within.

"We are here to right the ultimate wrong," she said. "Birth! If there's some Almighty with any grace out there, we're none but his angels."

With his eyes on the side mirror, Micah reversed down the drive. Darkness and solitude crept over the death house, sealing it away as he and Mama departed for whatever conjunction awaited in the distance of the night.

***

"Dad!" Jessica shouted. "Dad!"

Part of her knew, on a rational level, that there were a hundred good reasons that could explain why her father wasn't back yet. Another part knew, instinctively, that something was wrong. Something had to be wrong, otherwise he would have come back already. He wouldn't leave her and Mom alone at night in the middle of nowhere. He wouldn't make the kind of mistake she had made, the mistake that had cost Billy his life.

"Dad!" she called again, her voice broken by tears.

A faint light appeared in the center of the horizon. The light split into two orbs which steadily grew in size as they flew through the sleeping abyss. Soon they were joined by the buzz and occasional coughs of an engine.

Jessica walked towards the headlights and waved her hands.

"Dad!"

The headlights stopped moving toward her. Jessica realized the vehicle had come to a stop. Then the headlights died, and black night sucked the road - and Jessica - into its maw.

Cold air crawled on Jessica's arms. She could hear the motor running as the vehicle idled in the road. Then the engine growled as the vehicle slowly started moving forward again.

Jessica stopped walking. Her breath caught in her throat. She listened to the crunching of gravel as the car crept slowly toward her. Despite the canopy of branches that hung over the road, there was enough filtered moonlight that Jessica was soon able to see the approaching vehicle clearly, a small truck or camper van, its box-like body painted black.

The sight of the van made her pull back

from the road and into the forest, where deeper night hung beneath the trees and the ground was a morass of dead leaves.

The van continued its slow approach. Jessica hid behind a tree, hugging the trunk so tight the bark poked into her side. The camper drew level with her hiding place, and came to a stop. Jessica peered around the side of the tree so cautiously she could barely see anything.

The passenger door opened and the sight of the emerging figure knocked the air out of Jessica's lungs like a physical strike. It looked like a naked female, but dark and disfigured, an extra set of twisted limbs dangling on its torso, as though it were a mutant fetal specimen released from its jar and given a second chance to live and grow. Jessica tried to make out more details, but the shadows around the figure were too thick. Whatever the thing was, it crept in pace with the van as the vehicle once again began to slowly advance down the road towards the RV.

From her hiding place Jessica kept her eyes trained on the figure and the van. She almost cried out as a beam of moonlight illuminated the scythe in the hands of the stalking figure, then the figure itself, a naked woman black with gore and wearing a pair of severed arms like a loose-fitting scarf.

Jessica's eyes went instinctively to the RV.

Her silent prayer remained behind her teeth.

Mom, please, Mom!

The van rolled on towards the RV. For a time the naked woman kept pace beside it, then sped towards the RV like a ghost in the moonlight. The scream that erupted from her throat brought tears to Jessica's eyes. The woman was praying too, only to a different God - a strange, malevolent God invoked with barbarian chants.

Guilt began to build in Jessica's chest. She couldn't stay hidden, couldn't abandon Mom to that woman with the scythe. With a racing heart she followed the woman and the van, flitting from shadow to shadow, avoiding the moon's cold glare.

The woman with the scythe maintained her swift pace, reaching the RV way before Jessica, and way before the dark van, which continued to slowly drag itself along.

Jessica dashed into a shadow closer to the RV. Should she scream and warn Mom? How many other freaks were inside that van, other than the woman with the scythe? As her frantic mind ran through the possibilities, she felt something hard sting her thigh from inside her pocket.

The keys!

The realization came with a sigh of relief. She'd locked the door to the RV when she'd gone to look for dad. Whoever these people were, they wouldn't get inside the vehicle without a fight. She was out here, unseen in the darkness. She had the momentum.

The van stopped again, while Jessica kept moving, keeping to the darkness of the woods parallel to the road. She pulled the keys from her pocket and grasped them so that the largest one poked out from between her index and middle fingers like a punch dagger.

The terrain between her and the RV was now only thickets and long grass. There were no more trees to hide behind. But she was almost behind the woman with the scythe. If she kept herself low, she could close the short distance in cover.

The woman had slowed her pace and was now at the back of the RV, inspecting the dark rear windows. Jessica crouched and began to crawl through mud and withered grass towards the woman. Then a soft thud stopped Jessica in her tracks.

She raised her head towards the sound and saw that the van had stopped once again. The front seats were empty, and a slim figure stood by the driver's side door. A boy in outline, his face a black void blocked from the moonlight.

The woman turned towards the camper and the boy. In the momentary stillness, in the nocturnal light, Jessica got a better look at the woman, and at the arms that dangled from her neck, complete with twisted fingers and rings that glinted in the moonlight - a wedding ring, a college ring - *Dad's rings.*

Jessica clenched the keys so hard they cut into her palm.

Dad!

She made another silent prayer. A prayer of violent despair aimed at whatever abomination would listen. The blood from her fingers dripped into the mud as if to seal the deal.

She was in hell. If there was any deliverance to be found in the universe, it was long overdue, and probably not coming. All she asked for was enough fuel for her vengeance.

***

The white RV shone in the moonlight, three times the length of Mama's van and almost twice as tall. Each darkened window was the size of the van's windshield. But Micah didn't let the grandeur of the vehicle distract him from his task. He and Mama were expecting a family, just as the man had said. There was no telling how many souls sheltered beyond those black windows. He placed a palm on the hilt of his knife and felt the reassuring weight of the gun tucked into his pants against the small of his back.

The darkness around them shifted and thickened as the moon tried to hide its face behind a tattered blanket of clouds. Mama went back into the van and came out holding the man's severed head in her hands. His eyes seemed to stare in horror at the scene. Mama raised the head to sniff the exit wound, then moved back towards the motor home.

"Come," she said.

Something moved behind the dark windows. Micah reached behind his back and took hold of the pistol grip. He could just make out the fuzzy image of someone moving down the length of the RV towards the center. A moment later the automatic door pushed outwards with a faint mechanical noise and began to slide aside.

A woman in a white nightgown stepped outside and faced them. Mama sank into a slight crouch as if ready to pounce. The woman saw the severed head in Mama's hands and froze.

"Philip?" she said. "Philip. Philip!"

The name became an alien shriek on her tongue. Micah felt it deep inside himself. He pulled his knife and strode toward her. He had to be fast.

The woman didn't look away from her dead husband's face until Micah grabbed her by the hair and yanked her head back. That's when their gazes met. Her eyes were deep with sorrow, nought but black wounds seeping. The same darkness Micah wanted to remove from himself oozed from her skull.

The woman trembled, and Micah eased his grip instinctively. For the first time he understood. This woman didn't want to hurt them. None of the girls - none of the dead - had wanted to hurt them. Suddenly he saw it all clearly - his mother's lies, his own regret, the true face of the nameless abhorrence that clawed at his heart.

The woman fell back onto him. He tried to push her off but she was too heavy, too limp. He lost his footing and fell backward. The vista of the forest became a blur of stars. His head slammed into the soil and for a second the world went dark. When the light returned he saw the woman atop him. Her twitching body pinned him down; a black hole in her head stared at him like a third eye.

Mama stood next to them both, her blade dripping dark.

Micah could barely move his legs. The pistol tucked into his pants pressed into the small of his back like a rock. He managed to remove it and toss it aside. Meanwhile the woman's head poured blood onto his chest like an overturned cup.

Mama let out a snarl and vanished from his field of vision. He craned his neck and saw her lying on the side of the road. There was someone else, someone on top of Mama, beating her.

Micah tried to push himself up, but the dead woman was too heavy. He tried to slide himself out from under her, but only managed to move himself a little.

Meanwhile Mama fought her way back to her feet. The dead man's arms had fallen from around her neck. She hissed like a snake and clawed the face of her attacker.

The attacker stumbled backward. Micah saw it was a young woman. Mama pushed her down and pinned her to the ground with a knee against her throat.

The woman gurgled and raked at Mama's legs. Her lower body thrashed. Mama reached for her scythe, which lay on the ground between her and Micah. Micah tried to grab it to throw it to her, but it was just beyond his reach. His fingers strained toward the handle, but it was no good. He couldn't escape the dead woman's weight. His legs were numb now, filled with pins and needles.

Mama leaned out further, her own fingers striving for the blade. The girl thrashed just as Mama's balance was at its weakest. Mama fell down on all fours, her knee slipping off the girl's neck, her outstretched hand landing on the handle of her scythe. The girl slipped out from under her and grabbed her by the hair, pulling her face skyward. Mama turned to swing her scythe, but the girl struck first. Something flashed in the moonlight as her fist connected with Mama's left eye.

When the girl's fist drew back, Mama's eyeball was gone. Micah saw something poking out from between the girl's fingers, glistening and bloody. It was a long key.

The girl swung again and again, battering Mama's face. Black hollows and furrows opened up all over Mama's cheeks and eyes. She screamed and raised her hands in defense, but it was no use. The girl kept striking, shredding her visage. Mama fell into a fetal ball and clutched at her gouged-out eyes. The girl stepped away from her and picked up the scythe.

Micah fought to get free. Desperate for leverage, he sank one of his thumbs through the hole in the dead woman's skull and yanked at her head. Pushing her shoulder with his other arm, he managed to roll her onto one side, freeing one of his legs, while the other remained trapped beneath her bulk.

The girl swung the blade with both hands. It flashed down through the air like a descending column of lightning. Mama's head shook from the impact. The fingers clutching at her face were hacked away. So was her nose. Screaming, the girl swung again and again, chopping into Mama's head as if she were trying to cut through a log.

Micah dragged his other foot free. He scrambled to his feet and away from the dead woman, limping from the numbness in one of his legs. He could hear his heart pounding in his ears. Black spots dotted his vision and his skull ached where he'd struck it on the ground. For a moment his vision faded to almost nothing. He stopped for a moment and focused on breathing.

The world became visible again. A silver crescent shone in the night before him. It was the edge of the barrel of his own gun, pointed towards him. Standing behind it was the girl from the dead man's wallet, her hair and face red with blood.

"Shit," she said. "You look just like him."

Micah stared back at her. Her tears turned red as they rolled down her cheeks. There was a strange grace in her eyes, and for a moment her gaze seemed to wash away his pain, as though he were a blade licked clean. The girl pulled the trigger.

"I'm so sorry," she said.

FIN

BRIMSTONE

Amy positioned a pillow under her mother's head. The smell of the sick woman's medicines tainted everything with their bitterness, even her breath and sweat. She needed a bath, but Amy didn't have time; she couldn't leave Tom hanging for the third night in a row. She glanced at the clock on the wall. It, too, seemed to be suffering; its smallest hand trembled like a dying spider struggling to climb.

Mom spoke through the transparent oxygen mask. "You're...going...somewhere?"

"I won't be out long."

"Stay...as long...as you like. I'm not... going anywhere...yet." Mom gave her a weak smile.

"You want me to put the TV on?"

"I'm okay."

Amy fetched the remote and placed it on the desk beside the bed. She checked the oxygen tank and saw the meter was still in the green. "Do you want water or anything?"

Mom closed her eyes. "I said...I'm fine."

Amy gave her a quick kiss on the cheek, then headed for the door. "See you soon," she said.

Mom coughed. "D...darling? Turn the lights off, please."

Amy flipped the switch and the room went dark.

***

Nocturnal suburbia stretched across the valley, a sea of shadowy lawns split by roads and strings of yellow light. Amy sat on her sedan's hood and lit a smoke. The autumn breeze teased goose pimples from her skin. The howl of a siren rose above the buzz of crickets, then was drowned by the roar of an engine climbing the hill behind her.

"Finally."

Glaring headlights mounted the hill and a car pulled in beside hers with a screech. A voice she didn't like came through the car's open window. The accent was pure toothless white trash. "He's not here yet?"

"Didn't expect you, Will," said Amy, hating the fact she knew this creep's name.

Will shrugged his bony shoulders. The feeling of dislike was clearly mutual. He emerged from the car and loitered uncomfortably close to her. "How's your mom?"

Amy took a drag of her smoke. Not even the rich tobacco haze could cover the fact that Will lived in some abandoned hellhole without running water. The guy stank. She wished Tom had a dealer whose mouth didn't smell like roadkill.

She peered into the distance with no intention of answering Will's question. The less he knew about her, the better. A guy like this would rob her house the second he found out about her Mom's heavier medications.

"Where's Tom?" she asked, growing impatient.

Will lit a smoke. "I just asked your man a little favor. He'll be here soon."

Amy wondered what Will meant by "A little favor."

Will nodded towards the woods. "Here he is."

Tom emerged from the shadows of a trail mouth and headed straight to Will. Will handed him a dime bag, then got into his car and started the engine. "See you two around." He pulled his car out and shot Amy a glance that made her uncomfortable.

She waited till his headlights vanished into the dark. "Okay, what was that about?"

Tom glanced around, as if to make sure no one was watching, then showed her the dime bag and the handful of black powdery pills inside. "This is special stuff."

"Special, huh?" She stared at the pills. "What did you have to do to get them? Will said some kind of favor."

Tom tucked the pills back into his pocket. "It was nothing, don't worry about it. Not even anything illegal. Guy's just a weirdo, that's all. Almost feel like I'm taking advantage of him." He placed his hands on her shoulders and ran them down her cold arms. "God, ain't you freezing?"

Amy ignored his question. "I don't like that Will guy. Don't leave me hanging out with him alone again, okay?"

"Sure thing, babe. Won't happen again."

She lifted her heels and rested them on the front bumper. Tom pressed himself close. "I've still got those leftover pills from Friday, the Tweeties. Want one?"

Amy blew smoke into his face. "Not tonight, but you can give me something else."

Tom's eyes focused on Amy's lips. He pressed her down against the car hood. Amy threw her cigarette away and reached for his crotch, pulling his zipper open. She slipped a hand inside his jeans. As Amy stroked him, she stared up at the indifferent stars, looking for a pattern.

***

Amy peered into Mom's room. The steady hiss of oxygen filled the dark, punctuated by heavy breaths. Leaving the door ajar, Amy crept to the living room and sat on the couch that served as her bed. She reached for a backpack on the floor and pulled out The Black Codex. Golden sigils on the cover shone, even where no light seemed to fall, and the leather felt warm and almost damp, like the skin of a perspiring beast.

Amy's interest in the occult had been growing for years. At her age people usually embarked on ambitious careers or made children to distract them from the harsh and inevitable passage of time. Not so for Amy.

Others tried to deny the darkness gnawing at them, but Amy prided herself on seeking instead to understand it - even to embrace it. Thus she had sought out the Codex, whose central focus - one might even call it a doctrine - was the long-lasting tradition of selling one's soul to the Devil.

She had already performed the first ritual. Last week, she had climbed the vine-covered wall into the cemetery and crossed into the oldest section, where the ancient dead sprawled in triumphant decay.

Her spine shivered with excitement. Walking the avenues and paths, Amy passed countless monuments commemorating the once great and powerful, now stripped of their glory and crowns.

Onwards she continued, into the very innermost part of the cemetery, where the shadows seemed deeper, the statues even more towering and ancient. Here she found a grove of trees nestled between the mausoleums, sinister even against the backdrop of the necropolis. In the center was a bald spot, above which the branches of dead trees formed a canopy like withered hands in prayer.

Amy knelt and raked the earth with bare hands until she had created a miniature grave. With cemetery dirt beneath her nails, she spoke the words of The Black Codex.

"As I make my bed in Hell, behold, thou art there."

Amy took six black coins and placed them at the bottom of the pit.

"Hail Satan."

She covered the spot and meditated, feeling the night's black claws carve a sense of surging power into her heart. She knew now it was only a matter of time.

As she headed back, Amy noticed the maples along the grand avenue had grown since her last visit. How long had it been? Thirteen years? Thirteen years, and she still remembered exactly where Jimmy was buried. The passing of time meant nothing. The memory would stay with her like a stubborn stain that could never be washed away. Faded maybe, but always there.

***

Lillian sat on her bed and touched the photo of her dead husband Harry. She thought about death - or rather, of a person's relationship with death. She thought about it as a spiral one walks from the inside outwards, each revolution a different phase of life. First abstract fears; then the solid grief of burying loved ones; then the daily rebellion of one's own body. And that's where she was right now. In strange flesh. Turning to dust. Just like Harry...

She dragged her heavy legs into bed and turned off the lamp. Moonlight bled into the room through the blinds. All was still, and then -

Something rustled in the hall. Lilian turned towards the sound but could see only darkness beyond the door. She felt a breeze brush her exposed skin.

"You old fool," she muttered."Forgot to lock the door again..."

She reached for the switch on the base of her bedside lamp, then froze. A figure was there in the doorway, almost hidden by the shadows.

"You," she said. "What's this about?"

No answer. The figure remained still. The features were hard to make out, but the build told her it was a man, with something long grasped in his hands.

The figure launched itself on top of her and smashed her skull against the headboard. Lilian couldn't see the iron rod, could only hear the faint whisper of air as the weapon sped down to meet her face. Without being conscious of her journey, Lillian exited the spiral.

***

Amy woke to her phone beeping. A text from Tom read:

Wanna take a few pills tonight? Miss you babe

Amy put the phone down and yawned.

"Mom, are you awake?"

No answer. Amy headed to her mother's bedroom, stretching her stiff joints on the way. Mom was awake but silent; she waved Amy inside. Amy went in and raised the blinds to allow the pale light of morning in.

"Pray...with me...dear?" said her mother through her mask.

"Sure," Amy said even though it was the last thing she wanted to do this morning.

Amy knelt by the bed and took her mother's gaunt hand in hers. As Mom prayed, Amy watched the clock. If she were to pray, she would ask for

Mom to be cured, or at least mercifully taken off to another place. Anything other than this slow demise, this clinically-monitored Golgotha. How could medicine keep a person alive for so long, in so much misery?

Every part of the process made Amy sick. The smell of the hospital hallways. The lime green paint in the waiting rooms. The twitching hands of the clocks. Every hour her mother lived on was not a gift, but a curse from the most vehement God Amy could imagine.

Mom's prayer was indecipherable as usual. Perhaps she kept the words from Amy's ears in the superstitious belief that a hidden prayer had more power.

Finally the "Amen" came, and Amy stood up.

"I'm...sorry, dear," said her mother. "I know it's...a bit of a pain..."

"It's alright," said Amy. "Come on, let's get you cleaned up."

Amy pulled back the sheets. The acrid smell of urine washed over her.

Mom staggered to the bathroom without assistance. This wasn't the first time Mom had been incontinent and surely wouldn't be the last. The linen would have to be changed, and the mattress cover cleaned and aired. Amy would put the incontinence pads on her tonight, whether Mom wanted them or not.

"You okay?" Amy yelled towards the bathroom.

"Yes," said Mom.

"I'll be there in a minute."

Ever since the cancer had spread from Mom's lungs to her brain, she'd been increasingly confused and forgetful. Every time Amy left her alone she ran the risk of something going wrong.

Amy began to strip the bed, then sat and pressed her thumbs into her aching temples.

"Fuck it," she whispered.

Things couldn't go on like this. It was still morning but she was already craving the Double F. The only true intervention she knew. A fuck and a fix — a cocktail of the gods.

***

The washing machine ate Amy's coins as eagerly as the graveyard had. She walked into the light drizzle outside the laundromat and lit a cigarette. She thought about mainstream "magick" and scoffed. Such a hard, roundabout way of achieving the mundane. Why cast a love spell when the world was filled with strangers more than willing to fuck you? If you wanted something ordinary, all you had to do was make an effort. Want to lose weight? Just puke and stop eating. Want money? Sell your ass or rob a bank. But seeking something unusual, something primordial, demanded more. It demanded real magick - the magick of The Black Codex.

Amy couldn't wait to see how the process would strip her, how much filth there was to excavate from her sick self. The first ritual was an attempt to find a passage, a payment for the ferry. Her journey had begun - she could feel it - but she didn't know what to expect exactly. She just had to let the magick guide her, show her the signposts she couldn't ignore.

The drizzle transformed into lashing rain with thunder overhead. Amy pulled out her phone and began to text. Her need for the Double F was only increasing with the violence of the storm.

***

Amy dropped the fresh laundry in the hallway and stepped into the living room.

"Mom?" she called.

A shadow flitted across the crack beneath the bathroom door.

"Mom?" Amy called again. "I'm back."

She knocked on the door and heard a low

mumble from inside. She opened it and found the bathroom empty, the shower curtain fluttering as if in the aftermath of a sudden gust of wind.

A moan sounded behind her. She followed the sound into the bedroom. She saw her mother's legs first, splayed out on the floor, then her face with the blue-tinted lips.

"Mom!"

She rushed to her mother's frail form. She was still alive, still conscious, gasping ineffectively for air.

Instinctively Amy grabbed the oxygen tank and pressed the mask to her mother's mouth.

"Breath, Mom. Breathe."

She cranked the oxygen output. The tube hissed louder with each turn of the dial. Mom huffed. Amy held the mask in place while dialing 911 with her free hand.

Mom kept feebly clawing at her chest. Her rapid breathing didn't slow down. Her wide eyes stared into the distance as if she glimpsed some netherworld beyond the apartment walls.

"Help's on the way," Amy said. "Help is -"

The words died in her throat as she suddenly asked herself - was Mom clawing at the air to breathe, or to escape the cruel grip of life? She'd fought for so long, coming back from the brink again and again, until here she was, little more than a semi-conscious husk.

"Mom, you don't have to," said Amy, her grip slackening on the mask. "You can go. I'll be okay…"

Mom gripped Amy's wrist so hard her nails dug into the skin. Then her grip went slack and her eyes turned hazy.

"Mom!"

The ambulance arrived after what seemed like an eternity. As the wailing sirens escorted them to the hospital, neither Amy nor the paramedics knew if it was already too late.

***

Tom hurried down the street. Amy hadn't shown up for their date, nor had she answered her phone, but he had to find her, had to let her know what had happened. The day's headlines repeated in a feverish loop inside his head -

HUNT IS ON FOR SUSPECT IN BRUTAL SLAYING
QUIET SUBURB ROCKED BY SLAUGHTER
POLICE MOUNT SEARCH FOR GRANNY KILLER

Accompanying news articles showed images of a suburban house sealed by the police, where an 83-year-old woman had been found bludgeoned to death in her bed. Tom knew that house. He'd been there the previous night, following Will's instructions. Tom hadn't been inside, only in the backyard, and only for a minute, burying a black nail in the soil. He'd pushed that strange object into the ground, but he hadn't harmed anyone. As for what Will had done, that was a whole other question. What if Will had killed that old woman? He might try to pin it on Tom, or name him as an accomplice, even though he hadn't done anything.

As Tom headed into Amy's apartment complex, he couldn't shake the feeling everyone was looking at him. The sensation was suffocating.

He found Amy's apartment and was about to ring the bell when he saw the door was already ajar. He pushed it open and stepped inside.

"Amy?" His voice echoed in the hall. "Anyone home?"

Amy's tired voice came from the living room. "Tom? Hey, in here."

Tom went in and saw her sitting in the dark.

"Mom's in the ICU," Amy said.

Tom sat beside her and stroked her hand. "You want to go see her?"

"No, I was just there. She's stable, so they sent me home for the night. I'll go back in the morning, unless..." her voice trailed off.

Tom didn't know what to say. Everything seemed to be crumbling. He felt doomed, as if the gods had tied the string of his fate into a noose.

"You still got those black pills with you?" asked Amy, interrupting the loop of anxious thoughts spinning through Tom's head.

Her timing was bad, but Tom couldn't say no. "Will calls them Brimstone," he said. "There's something weird about 'em but I'm not really sure what…"

"Well, weird or not, I could use some right about now."

Tom pulled the dime bag from his pocket and handed it to her. She studied the pills through the plastic.

"There's something important I need to tell you," he said.

Amy gave him her attention, but he hesitated, unsure how to proceed. He didn't want to add to her stress, but she needed to know. "I think Will's in some deep shit," he said. "And I might have something to do with it."

He took out his phone and showed her the news app. Her eyes widened as she scanned the article and the horrendous details it contained. She finished reading and handed him the phone back. Tom filled the silence with anxious words.

"Will gave me this thing, this big black nail with writing on it, weird writing, like some kind of foreign shit, and asked me to do him a favor in exchange for those Brimstone pills. He said all I had to do was stick the nail in the ground of some backyard. I went out and chose the first house I came to. I stuck the nail in and left. I thought he was just being crazy, cooked in the head from too much meth, but..." Tom pointed at the photo on the news app. "It was that same house. It was dark, but I'm sure of it. If anyone finds out I was there last night, I'm fucked."

Amy placed a hand on his forearm. "You need to calm down. You're freaking out."

Tom nodded and tried to force himself to relax.

Amy took a pill out of the dime bag.

"Maybe we should -"

She swallowed the whole pill before Tom could say only take half.

"So you went there and buried a nail in the backyard and left?" she said. "And then this murder happened inside the house?"

Tom nodded. "Yes, and—"

"And you have no idea about any of it?"

"No, I don't. I swear. But I'm sure Will does."

"Then what's there to worry about? You didn't actually do anything wrong. Just because you were in the backyard doesn't mean shit. You don't know anything about any murder. Chill out."

Tom nodded in silent agreement. He wanted to believe her, that nothing more would come of this.

Amy sat on his lap and slipped a black pill between his lips. Tom took it. He couldn't help but get aroused from the feeling of her body against his, despite the acrid taste of the pill dissolving in his mouth and the nagging fear that his days of freedom might be numbered.

Amy ground herself against him and placed a hand on his hardness. They tasted the bitterness of the pills as they kissed.

Tom knew this was where he belonged. Amidst all the chaos, all the fear, this was relief.

Amy threw off her shirt and offered her breast to his lips. As he sucked she moaned and undulated like a witch at a Black Sabbath dance. He slid his finger into her cleft, pouring gasoline on her fire. They fucked like the world was coming to an end.

***

Amy shivered, happily spent after multiple orgasms. Bite marks dotted her skin. She lay on the floor with Tom, their sweaty bodies pressed against each other.

Tom kissed her temple. "You want a family some day?"

Amy didn't answer. She had no desire to pass on her diseased DNA.

Tom didn't press the issue. In silence, he caressed her neck.

Amy stared at the ceiling, where indistinct shapes writhed in the shadows like worms in the earth. Wet rot oozed through the flimsy illusion of the apartment walls as if dripping from some cosmic mass grave just beyond the reach of her senses.

Amy reflected on the ritual she had performed, her profound hate for the Creator. She thought about the nail Tom had placed in that backyard. She too had placed pieces of metal in the earth, a gesture to initiate a pact, open a path. Was there a common thread?

"Why did Will get you to do that? Put that nail in the ground?" she asked.

"Some ritual, I guess," said Tom. "Will's crazy, you know? But it was important to him. So important he gave me the Brimstone in exchange."

Amy said nothing. Graveyard voices whispered in her ears. She loved being high. Who wouldn't, when the tapestry of fate itself appeared through the prism of intoxicated dreams?

She caressed Tom's sweaty chest. "Wanna get outta here?"

"Sure, where?"

"To find Will and figure this shit out, once and for all."

Tom stayed silent as she got up and slipped into her clothes.

Amy felt a sinister triad of forces leading her down a path she couldn't refuse. Black coins, black pills, a black nail in the earth. Onward she would go, into the vortex. And Tom would come along for the ride.

***

When Amy was young her parents had tried for another child. Her mother always said that if they had another girl they would name her Becka. Amy liked to imagine what Becka would be like. What kind of hair she would have, what kind of candy she'd like, what kind of games she'd play. She talked about Becka all the time, as if she were already a part of the family, and was simply waiting to be born.

When she was six, Amy's father put an end to the fantasy.

"You have no sister, and you never will. So I want you to stop talking about it."

He slammed his fist on the table. Amy broke into tears. Mom sat silently, her eyes downcast. They finished their dinner without further words and went to bed. The next morning her father got up early, left for work, and never came back.

Mom began to pray a lot after that. She'd beg the Lord Jesus to help them, but he never did. Listening to her mother pray, Amy always got the feeling she'd taken something away from her parents when she'd been born, something she'd give back if only she knew how. Broken dreams, ruined plans, all the things that might have survived if she'd never existed.

When her mother prayed for Amy's father to return, for his heart to soften, Amy understood the unspoken subtext of the prayer: that her parents' broken dreams and ruined plans would be mended, that things would go back to how they'd been before Amy had been born, that Amy herself would somehow be erased.

And so when Mom prayed, Amy imagined Jesus coming down from heaven to cast her into Hell and finally grant her parents peace. This image made Amy fear Jesus and tremble in dread every time his name was invoked. Night after night she would awaken, soaked in sweat from nightmares of a kidnapping Christ.

One night, Amy awoke from yet another hellish vision, filled with the sense of something evil pursuing her. Her mother told her to be quiet, but Amy couldn't stop screaming until a hard slap across the face silenced her cries.

Amy's mother switched off the light and left the room without a word.

Amy pulled the blanket over her head. In the darkness of her soft makeshift cave, she thought about Jesus in a whole new light. She was no longer scared of the kidnapping Christ. She wanted him to come and take her away.

After that night, Mom took to praying alone in her room with the door closed. Amy could only make out faint whispers through the wall. Time passed and Jesus didn't seem to answer any of her prayers. Maybe something more drastic was needed, Amy thought, something that would force him down from the heavens. A sacrifice? A death?

***

The Subaru's headlights cut through a pocket of deep darkness as Tom turned off the main highway and onto a country road. He checked the rearview, unable to shake his paranoia, but there was no one behind them.

Amy watched the landscape speed past. Scattered houses gave way to pure forest.

Could Will really have done it, she wondered? Murder? The word dripped with intoxicating finality. There was something transcendent, even inhuman about it. There was no way to set oneself apart from mankind so fundamentally than by immersing one's hands in the bloody work of death. But that was something Amy already knew about.

Tom parked in a patch of weeds on the edge of the woods. Amy got out. The air was brisk; she could hear the trickle of a river somewhere nearby.

"Christ, I didn't know he lived way the fuck out here," she said more to herself than to Tom.

Tom took a flashlight from under the driver's seat and joined her outside. "It's about two miles in," he said. "Will gets paranoid if anyone drives too close to the house."

"Huh, great. I guess we're walking then." Amy said, feeling she didn't have much of a choice if she wanted answers. Black coins, black pills, black nail in the earth - a force was drawing her toward Will even though she loathed him.

They stepped over dying grass onto a trail that led into the woods. The air grew moist, infused with the scent of conifers and moss. For a while the trail ran alongside the river, then split from it and led towards the base of a nearby mountain. Twisted roots had wound themselves through wounds in the earth. Beneath the pall of shadow, they seemed to move like serpents.

Tom mounted an incline and helped Amy up after him. They pressed on. A cloud of foreboding hung about them. The creatures of the forest remained mute and unseen, as if shying away from the foreign presence tainting their home. They passed overturned trees that dotted the hillside like the remains of ancient sacrificial altars.

Amy's sense of shapeless oppression intensified. They came upon a dead tree with the vague shape of a twisted human body, overgrown with weeds and moss. Something about it struck a chord with Amy, a sense of deja vu, as though she were hearing a song from childhood, or glimpsing the face of a long-lost friend. A rancid smell drew her attention to the base of the trunk, where maggots crawled across the carcass of a rotting, crucified raccoon.

Tom drew back in disgust, but Amy stepped closer, entranced. She peered into the gaping remains. For a moment she felt as if she were tumbling out of her body, down into the largest and darkest of the wounds, past the maggots and the frayed edges to someplace beyond.

Amy closed her eyes and clung to the sense of peace the darkness offered her, trying to nurture it inside herself. She wasn't afraid. She knew it was Holy, a signpost on the path she had opened for herself with that first ritual in the cemetery.

She felt the darkness stir inside her as she followed its urging. Soon she would have her transcendence - in one form or another.

***

"Amy?" Tom took her shoulder and shook it gently.

"What?" she said, finally looking away from the stinking carcass.

"Maybe we should turn back?" he said, feeling nervous all over again. Will wasn't the kind of guy who appreciated surprise guests or direct confrontation.

"What?" she said. "Are you serious? No way!"

"Well yeah, I..." his voice trailed off as her blank stare bored into him.

"Tom, listen to me," she said. "We already talked about this in the car. If we don't do something, you could end up in prison. You said it yourself, Will has too much dirt on you. Do you think you can pull me into this, get this whole thing started, and then just backflip and walk away? Will's got you by the throat. You better be ready."

"Ready for what?"

"To see this fucking through," she said, the look in her eyes turning ugly. "Do you think Will's gonna let you walk away from all this? Do you think he's not gonna try and use you somehow? Stop being so fucking weak."

Tom didn't answer.

Amy pulled a folding knife from her pocket. She flicked open the blade and peered at its gleaming edge with an intensity Tom had only ever seen her exhibit during sex.

"Let's move," she said. "We'll settle the score together."

"Are you fucking serious?" Tom said, staring at the knife. "Do we really need that?"

Amy shrugged. "I just wanna make sure it's us who walk out of all this, if it comes down to that."

"It won't," said Tom.

They pressed on. Tom couldn't shake the eerie feeling he was walking with a stranger.

***

Amy had learned from the preacher man on TV that one had to do evil and then die to go to Hell. She saw pictures of Hell, where naked people screamed in flames, surrounded by demons with cruel-looking weapons and limbs from different types of animals. She saw drawings of people swimming in big pots over fires, and tried to imagine the hotness of Hell as the hottest possible bath a person could take. She wanted to go there, but she was so young, and death felt so far away. Growing old would take forever. In the meantime, she had to deal with her mother every day.

Each night, Amy would pray "Dear Jesus, send me to Hell. Dear Jesus, send me to hell. Dear Jesus..."

But Jesus didn't answer. She knew he wanted something more than just words. An offering, like the one Cain had made of Abel.

She found her chance one day when she was playing in her backyard and heard a rhythmic thumping sound coming from the patio of the nice house next door. She peered through the hedgerow separating the yards and saw little Jimmy bouncing his ball.

"Why are you spying on me?" he said.

"Do you know who Jesus is?" she asked.

Jimmy shaded his face from the sun. "What?"

"Do you know who Jesus is?" she asked again.

"Sure I do. That's a stupid question."

"Do you know what he looks like?"

"Of course."

"You ever seen him in person?"

He laughed. "No."

"How do you know what he looks like, then?"

Jimmy bounced the ball absentmindedly. "I've seen pictures."

"You wanna see him for real?"

"You're crazy," said Jimmy, focusing his attention back on the ball.

"No I'm not. You said you've never seen him, but I can show you. I know how to make him appear."

Jimmy tossed the ball into the grass. He glanced at the windows of his house and saw no movement inside; his Mom was probably still napping away her migraine. With a shrug, he stepped through the hedgerow into Amy's backyard.

"How do we bring him?" he asked.

Amy said nothing. She led Jimmy into her empty house. Her mother had gone to pick up groceries, and wouldn't be back for at least an hour. Jimmy followed her into her bedroom, where Amy removed her dress.

"Time to play Hell," she said.

Jimmy stared at her naked body in silence.

"You have to be naked too," Amy said. "People are always naked in Hell."

Jimmy said nothing.

"Jesus won't come if you don't undress."

Jimmy avoided her gaze. "We're not supposed to—"

"Just do it," she said.

Jimmy took off his T-shirt. Amy encouraged him to keep going.

"We're not going to tell anyone," she said.

Keeping his eyes downcast, Jimmy kicked off his shoes and pulled down his pants. Amy led him into the bathroom and told him to wait by the tub. She went downstairs to the utility drawer and returned with duct tape and scissors.

Jimmy looked at the objects in her hands. "What're those for?"

She placed the scissors atop the toilet seat and began peeling the tape off the roll. "Jesus won't come unless we do it the right way." She cut off a generous length of tape and rolled it snuggly around Jimmy's wrists. Jimmy gave the binding a perplexed look, but didn't resist as Amy bound his ankles in a similar fashion. Next, Amy stepped into the bathtub.

"Come on, you have to get in," she said, and awkwardly helped him into the tub.

Once he was in, Amy climbed out and let him lie flat. She went to her room and pulled her demon mask from under the bed. She'd coated it with stark red paint the color of Hellfire. She put on the mask and returned to the bathroom.

"What's that?" said Jimmy when he saw her.

"Take it off."

Amy left the mask on. Jimmy got into the spirit of the game by sitting up and trying to escape from the tub. Amy shoved him onto his back.

"Let me go!" he said. "I don't want to play anymore."

She held him down and taped his mouth shut. He was starting to look like a damned soul, his eyes wide with fright. He struggled like a worm beneath her weight as she pushed him flat against the enamel of the deep, claw-foot tub.

"Jesus, take us to Hell," she said.

Jimmy tried to add some words of his own, but the tape muffled his cries.

Amy reached over Jimmy and turned on the red tap, then jumped back from the torrent of water. "Jesus, come!" she ordered.

Steam rose up from the Hell Pot, fogging the mirror and filling the room. Jimmy moaned in pain through the duct tape, for the water was already close to boiling point, thanks to a faulty thermostat Amy's father had never bothered to fix before he had left. Wherever the water touched him, Jimmy turned red. In moments he was crimson all over his crotch, belly, and thighs. He thrashed and recoiled in agony, splashing hot droplets all over the room.

"Jesus, come!" shouted Amy again, while

Jimmy struggled to rise in the tub. Amy had hoped his bound hands and feet would keep him in the Hell Pot, but to her dismay he was on his feet in moments, staring at her in pain and hatred, ready to slither over the edge of the tub like a worm to take shelter on the cool linoleum.

He was ruining the game.

"Get back in there!"

She pushed him backward. He smacked his head on the faucet and slid back into the tub under the cascade of burning water. His skin began to redden again, and blisters began to form, but Jimmy no longer wriggled or moaned. Instead he was still, a stream of blood - so much of it! - running from his head and down into the steaming, swirling vortex of the drain.

"Jimmy?"

There was no answer. The sacrifice had been made, though not in the way she'd intended. It was a few years later - after the incarceration, the therapy - that Amy realized she'd been praying to the wrong person all along.

***

Will had lit candles on the ground floor, transforming his decrepit Victorian lair into a maze of shadows dancing madly across rotten tapestries. Presently he sat in the center of the largest room, surrounded by a chalk circle he'd drawn on the dusty floorboards. Littering the room outside the circle, adorning the rotten panels of the walls, were talismanic markings he had made in an altered state of mind that now seemed utterly alien to him. Blood dripped from the truncated little finger of his right hand, severed just below the knuckle. The wound throbbed in time with his heartbeat, but at least the pain was mundane, ordinary.

What hadn't been ordinary was the way the severed finger had moved and wriggled of its own accord before he'd chopped it off and thrown it under the stairs.

He looked at the droplets of blood that dotted the chalk line, and his pulse quickened with mounting dread. Had the circle been compromised?

The darkness ahead of him thickened and oozed in ways not dictated by the movement of the candle flames. The wind howled through the mummified structures of the house. Out in the hallway, timbers creaked like a snarling beast. Will stood up and stared into the void.

He could just make out the sight of something approaching from the dark with slow, uneven movements. As it reached the edge of the light it stopped, and the sound of a hungry beast sniffing the air penetrated the flimsy walls.

Will lost control of his bladder. Warm piss flowed down his leg and across the chalk circle. As if in response, he heard the beast inhale. It smelled him and approached with the sound of claws scraping on floorboards.

For the first time, Will wished he'd chosen another path in life.

***

Tom and Amy continued to hike through the forest. In the halo of Tom's flashlight, the roots of the trees looked like veins in the flesh of a great dark god.

Finally, the trail intersected with a weedy gravel road. They paused at the fork of the paths. Amy placed a hand on the reassuring weight of the folding blade in her pocket. She felt something calling her, an open invitation made not with words, but with currents of sinister energy. Perhaps Tom could sense it too, at least on some level, for his breathing had grown tense, like that of an animal preparing for flight - or slaughter.

"Let's go," he said. "It's not far."

They trudged up the drive beneath a handful of weak stars.

The driveway was no more than two long scars in the grass. A three-story Victorian monstrosity half-hidden by the twisted shape of an oak tree loomed before them. Branches from the surrounding canopy fought for space with the mansion's black gables.

Amy stared at the house and sensed its magnetic significance. Immediately she knew this was the place she was destined to be, even if it was just a stepping stone on the path to her final destination.

She and Tom followed a series of uneven flagstones to the sagging front door. Paint yellowed by time hung in strips from the timber. Mold and moss were eating away at the gables.

Tom pointed through the front windows to a flicker of orange light. "He's home."

The hinges on the front door groaned as Tom pushed it open to reveal a hallway with a staircase on one side and shadowed doorways on the other. The stink of rot and chemicals impregnated the air.

"Shit," said Tom as his flashlight beam shone on something pale and bloody in the dust near the staircase. At first, it looked to Amy like a fat maggot, but as she drew closer she saw it was a severed finger. She drew her knife, keeping it at the ready.

"Amy," said Tom, his voice low and full of urgency. "Amy, look!"

She followed his gaze to the end of the flashlight beam, where a pair of stark white eyes peered from a face painted with gore.

"Will?" said Tom.

Will didn't answer. He stood in the doorway of the front parlor. Amy noticed the raw stump from which the finger on the floor had been carved.

Amy approached him slowly. "Will, what's going on?"

Still no answer.

Amy saw that his bare feet ended prematurely in a series of oozing stumps. His toes, like his finger, had been severed - but there was no sign of them.

Will retreated from the doorway into the room beyond. Amy and Tom followed.

"What the hell's going on?" said Tom as the beam of his flashlight swept the room, highlighting crude sigils drawn in chalk and accented with blood.

Amy shivered. It wasn't fear she felt, but a sense of contact with the forces she sought, the forces she'd conjured with the Codex. She looked at Will crouched silently in the corner of the room. His eyes were like black sinkholes. Through them she saw little Jimmy, bloody in the bathtub. She blinked and the image was gone.

"We need to talk," said Tom.

Will remained silent.

"Enough screwing around," said Amy. She flicked her blade open, letting its deadly glimmer add weight to her words. "Tell us about the old woman, Will. Tell us what you did to her."

Will raised his mutilated hand to cover his face. "I don't... know what you're talking about," he said, appearing dazed, as if he'd just been woken from sleep. "Who?"

Will seemed genuinely clueless, not just about the murder, but about his own numerous injuries.

Amy gestured to his shins, where the skin had been cut into noodle-like strips. "You might want to get that looked at," she said flatly.

Will looked down at his own mutilation, and started to scream.

"We need something," said Tom. "Something to bandage the wounds."

"Seriously?" Amy said, tired of acting like she cared.

***

Tom hurried into a back room and found

what he was looking for - a sleeping bag with a pile of clothes beside it. He reached into the heap and grabbed a black t-shirt with inverted crosses and distorted text printed on it.

Quickly he headed back down the hall toward the front parlor. He stopped as he saw something move from the corner of his eye, a shadowed figure that could have been animal, man - or something in between. Tom pointed his flashlight toward the space where it had been, but saw only swirling motes of dust.

"Tom, what the hell are you doing? Get in here already."

It was Amy's voice, jolting Tom from a trance he hadn't noticed himself falling into.

***

Will's injuries throbbed with agony.

"Here." Tom threw Will the black shirt.

Will pressed the rag to his wounds but felt little relief. Tom drew back and peered warily down the hallway he had come from.

Will laughed. "You seen it too, huh?"

Tom remained silent, but the fear in his eyes said it all.

"Seen what?" asked Amy.

Will ignored her and stared at the bloody

spectacle of his own mutilated feet. "Fuck," he said. "This house, you know, it ain't normal. Nothing's normal here." He coughed.

"Don't pass out," said Amy. "You still need to tell us what you did to that old woman."

"I don't know what you're talking about," Will mumbled.

Amy slapped him hard across the face.

"Show him," Amy said, turning to Tom. "Show him the news. Maybe it'll jog his memory."

Tom pulled his phone from his pocket and showed Will the news app. Will tried to read the headline but the letters blurred and lurched across his field of vision.

"Look at the photo," said Tom. "That's the house where I buried that nail for you."

The article was dated from that morning. Beneath the grim headline - HUNT IS ON FOR SUSPECT IN BRUTAL SLAYING - sat a photo of a house Will had no memory of ever seeing before. But what did he remember from last night? He'd gone into the woods and taken a lot of Brimstone. After that, everything was hazy. Was it possible? Had something happened during those dark, forgotten hours?

Will heard his dead uncle laugh somewhere in the darkness. A harsh voice whispered in his ear. *Don't you remember, boy?*

Images flashed into Will's consciousness, murky fragments exhumed from the depths of his mind. A dark living room. Framed photos on top of an old television. The stench of cleaner and medicine. A long hallway. White hair on a pillow. Dark blood pooled around a caved-in skull. The gurgling sound of air moving through a crushed trachea. Will's own hands and feet, baptized in the blood of another.

He had remained in the house for an hour afterward, clad in the old lady's gore, while his dead uncle barked from the darkness - *Blood for Satan, Willie my lad. Blood for Satan!*

And just like that, Will began to remember everything.

***

As Will stared vacantly, Amy began to pace the room in frustration. She felt so close to what she was chasing, but it was still just beyond her reach. Will wasn't giving her the knowledge she wanted, so she needed something else, a final push to help her unlock the door. The pills had helped her before, allowed her to glimpse through the rotting funeral pall of the universe. She held out an open hand to Tom. "Give me more."

Tom didn't seem to understand.

"The black pills, the Brimstone, or whatever," she said. "Give me the rest."

Tom handed her the bag. Amy popped the last two pills in her mouth. Will - who seemed to have suddenly regained his composure - smiled at the sight and whispered something under his breath.

"What did you say?" asked Amy.

"Brimstone," said Will. His laugh turned into a cough. "You two took all those pills, but you never asked what was in 'em. It's my uncle's recipe. Old magick mixed with modern chemistry. Ideal for calling up the Devil. You feelin' it now, aren't ya?"

Amy said nothing as she ground the last fragments of the bitter pills between her tongue and the roof of her mouth. Black pill, black coin, black nail in the earth. It was all linked, just as she'd thought all along.

Will turned to Tom, who stood in the doorway, peering fearfully into the dark as if waiting for the return of some fell beast.

"How 'bout you?" said Will. "You feelin' it yet? You seen it yet?"

"What?" said Tom, without taking his eyes off the darkness of the corridor.

"It," said Will. "Oh, it's around here somewhere."

Tom opened his mouth as if to speak - or to scream - but only a distorted murmur came out.

"Ok yeah," said Will. "You're seein' it, alright."

Tom stumbled backward as though he'd been struck by a charging ram. Amy saw nothing save a swirling of dust. Tom's body went stiff, then shook, as though he were struggling against invisible chains. He fell to his knees, grasping himself in a bear hug and clawing at his ribs.

"Tom!" said Amy. Before she could say another word - before she could move to his side - she felt the air thicken with a strange oppressiveness.

"In darkness, we're never truly alone," said Will.

Tom fell to his knees, black drool oozing from his mouth. Amy watched him convulse. Black bile splashed the floor in front of him. A bitter stench baptized the room. Tom looked up at her with a gaze of utter emptiness, as if all humanity had been scrubbed from his eyes.

"Tom?" Amy said, stepping backward.

He rose and ran at her without warning, ripping the knife from her hand and shoving her aside. Amy crashed to the ground alongside the discarded flashlight. The spinning beam illuminated Tom bearing down on Will. A series of metallic blurs flashed between them as Tom plunged the blade into Will's chest and abdomen over and over in a frenzy. Will moaned but didn't fight. Finally, Tom buried the blade in Will's chest and left it there.

Will twitched, a last spasm as he passed. But Tom wasn't done. He grabbed Will's carcass and gnawed at its throat with teeth stained black from Brimstone bile. His body shook as if with ecstasy. Amy watched the slaughter, unable to look away.

Tom finally dropped Will's lifeless remains and drew back to stare at his handiwork - the holes in Will's shredded body, the bite marks, his own bloody hands. A fleeting look of horror - of human conscience - marred the perfect emptiness of his eyes, then passed into oblivion, leaving nought but a reflection of the abyss. It was at that moment Amy knew; Tom was no longer there. She knew she should feel sorrow or pity for him, yet she could only stare in awe at the brutal eclipse of his soul; she could only rejoice in the manifestation of he whom she adored, he whom she had summoned in the graveyard beneath the funeral moon.

Amy dropped her pants and got down on all fours. "Fuck me."

Her body felt like it was splitting open with lust. She felt his hand claw her buttocks. She looked over her shoulder, and saw nothing human inside those eyes.

She'd never felt more alive.

***

Amy lit a cigarette. She lay on her side on the soiled floor, unable to sit due to the pain in her violated hindquarters. The sex had been brutal, bloody, agonizing - and yet, it was all she had craved, a true consummation of her midnight pact. She had felt his cold and thorny rod; she had kissed his ring; she had tasted his sacramental filth. Surely she was now His, and the world would be hers in return, just as the Codex had promised.

Will's corpse lay beside her; it had served as a gruesome prop throughout the hours of fornication. Amy glanced casually at the wrecked face and dead eyes, then tapped some ash into the wounds. Meanwhile Tom paced nearby. His humanity had returned, with predictable - and tedious - results.

"I had no choice," Tom said. "I had no choice." He kept repeating the phrase, then stared at Amy with imploring eyes. "You saw what happened! I had no choice, right?"

Amy shrugged and concentrated on trying to blow smoke rings. She didn't have much luck forming rings, but she did unleash a puff of smoke which looked a lot like a damned soul writhing in the flames of Hell. She watched it disperse with amusement.

"What the fuck?" said Tom. "How can you - how can you sit there, after everything, after..." Tom's voice trailed off. He looked utterly terrified, utterly exasperated.

Amy couldn't help but laugh.

"Fuck!" Tom let out a howl of rage and frustration, then stormed out of the house.

Amy's laughter died. She scrambled to her feet, wincing from the pain in her backside, and hurried after him, half-naked in the bursting light of dawn.

"Tom!" she shouted. "Tom, wait! You've got to give me a ride!"

Tom wasn't waiting. She caught a fleeting glimpse of him sprinting off down the drive and into the woods. In her current condition there was no way she could catch him.

Now it was her turn to curse.

"Fuck!"

She went back to the house and got dressed in the room with Will's corpse. The fresh morning light made the scene of carnage seem foreign somehow, even though she'd been wallowing in it all night. Once dressed, she searched the place and found a whole bag filled with dozens of Brimstone pills. She shoved it in her pocket, then pulled her soiled knife from Will's chest. She was about to leave, when a sudden impulse drew her back to Will's body.

"Another sacrament," she whispered, as she carved a chunk of meat from Will's thigh and slipped it between her teeth.

**

With a sigh of relief Amy trudged out of the woods and onto the side of the road. It had been a long walk, and she still had far to go.

I need a ride, she thought.

As if Satan had answered her prayer, Amy heard the roar of an approaching vehicle and stuck out her thumb. A red pickup decorated with rust and dried mud came to a stop a few feet ahead of her. An old man sat in the driver's seat, regarding her with saggy eyes.

Amy slipped into the passenger seat, and winced.

"You okay, young lady?" asked the driver.

"Oh, I'm fine, thanks," she said. "Just a bit sore from dancing all night."

"I remember what that was like," said the diver with a wink. He hit the gas and the trees on either side began to fly by. "Where you headed?"

"Just into -" she was about to say into town, when a sudden impulse told her to follow another path. "Just up here, to a friend's house. I'll show you where to stop."

"Sure thing, young lady."

The car sped on. Amy watched the road in silence until she spied a crossroads up ahead, where a desolate and overgrown-looking driveway split off from the main road and ran into the woods.

"This is it," she said. "Just up here."

The driver slowed to a stop and eyed the decrepit-looking road suspiciously. "I know these parts pretty good, I don't think anyone lives down there."

"That's where my friend said to meet her."

"You sure she's not pullin' your leg?"

Amy shrugged. "I hope not."

The old man looked worried. "Well, you gotta be careful around here. All kinds of crazy stories, 'specially about that old mansion, Satan's House..." He looked warily up the overgrown drive, then shrugged himself and nodded to her. "Well, off you go then, I guess."

"You think...you think you could drive me a little of the way down there? I think it'll be a bit far on foot." She gave him a pleading smile.

The old man melted. "Well, sure, I guess it won't make much of a difference to me."

He turned down the old path. Amy heard the rustle of tall grass and weeds against the car's undercarriage. The driver slowed to a crawl, wary of potholes and other hazards. At length they emerged into a weedy clearing where a derelict house sat boarded up and covered in graffiti. The old man squinted at it.

"See, I told you no one lives down here," he said. "This friend of yours -"

The old man's words were lost in a gurgle as Amy jammed her blade into his neck. It sank so deep her knuckles pressed into his jowls. She jerked the blade to slice through the airways and arteries. The driver's eyes bulged, reflecting the abandoned house. Amy yanked the blade free in a wide arc. Blood splattered the windows and a thick coppery smell filled the cabin.

The driver slumped. Amy trembled with an excitement so profound it turned into sickness. She purged a torrent of puke onto the floor between her feet, then lay back and closed her eyes, floating in a sea of euphoria. Finally she was one of the chosen few, one of the powerful ones, erased from the Book of Life, named in the Book of Death, baptized in the blood of one of His creations. The pact had been sealed.

She sat peacefully, drifting into a strange haze until the vibration of her mobile against her hip brought her back to her senses. She took the phone from her pocket and saw a missed call from Tom. She tapped the screen to call him back, only to arrive at his voicemail. Perhaps he had already destroyed his phone in a fit of paranoia. Which was a shame, because she wanted so much to tell him the wonderful thing she had just done. But would he care? Would he even understand? He had only ever been a vessel for the one she had truly desired, a cuckold to the force that had controlled him. Now he was back to just regular old Tom - dim, compliant, and doomed, just like Jimmy. There was no need to even leave him a message.

She terminated the call, put away her phone, and turned to the bloody man slumped against the steering wheel. Something about his posture reminded her of a penitent in church. But there would be no penitence for her, only the path she had chosen.

***

Amy woke to the sound of the apartment door opening and closing. How long had she slept? Hours, days? She had no idea. She sat up, feeling groggy, just as her mother stepped into the room.

"Mom? What are you doing back so soon?"

Mom was silent save for the wheeze of her labored breathing. She stared for a moment at the bag of Brimstone pills on the table, then shuffled off into her bedroom.

Amy followed after. "Mom! Answer me. What are you doing out of hospital? Last time I saw you, you could barely breathe!"

Amy's mother looked at her with exhausted eyes. "I just...wanted to...come home, that's all. You know...I hate hospitals."

"You left against their advice, didn't you?"

Mom said nothing, and Amy knew there was no point pushing the matter further.

"Do you wanna lie down?" she asked, moving into caregiver autopilot.

Mom nodded. Amy helped her onto the bed and placed a pillow under her head. There was a pregnant silence which seemed to swarm with the weight of things unsaid.

"Are you...happy, dear?" asked Mom. "I never...ask you...that."

Images flashed through Amy's mind - darting steel, knife wounds, sodomy, cannibalism, the sweet embrace of utter darkness. "Yes Mom," she said. "I'm truly happy now."

"That's good, dear," said Mom. "And that...

Tom boy. You…never let me meet him…is he…good to you?"

"Um, sure, he's great," she lied.

"That's…good, dear." There was a long pause filled with wheezing. "I know I've…been a great…burden to you, dear. And I know I wasn't…a great mother, when you were…young."

Amy said nothing. A mixture of sadness and rage tried to well up from some distant part of her, but she crushed it down. She was one of the chosen ones now, above the petty emotions of the herd.

"You going to pray now?" she asked, unable to keep the bitterness from her voice.

Mom shook her head. "I'm…done with prayers. I'm gonna meet…Him soon anyway." She wheezed, then looked Amy dead in the eyes. "I want to…go, Amy. Every day is agony. Please…help me." Pain punctuated her words, but she was beyond tears.

Amy stared at her for a minute. Images of black bile, death, and Brimstone flitted through her mind. Finally, she said "I can help you, Mom."

She left the room and returned with the bag of Brimstone.

"I suppose I don't…need to know…exactly what's in those."

"No, you don't," said Amy. "But these will

help you. Take you where you need to go."

Amy suppressed a cruel smile as she began to feed the pills into her mother's withered mouth one after another, until the bag was almost empty. She put the last few pills in her pocket, and watched. For a time the old woman just wheezed. Then her pupils grew wide, like black moons. She stared fixedly at the ceiling, a look of horror on her face, as though she were looking through the threadbare winding sheet of the universe, and glimpsing the truth that lay beyond; as though she were glimpsing Amy's beloved himself, the Prince of the Air, the God of this World.

Mom's eyes opened even wider. Then her whole body shook, black bile bubbled from her lips, and her spirit fled like a dying gust of wind from a piece of hung out laundry.

Once again, Amy felt a mix of sadness and anger well up from that forbidden vault of humanity inside of her. She crushed it down, but some of it escaped in the form of a single tear. She wiped it away with a sense of disgust. Feeling a need to excise her weakness - and take another dark sacrament - she unfolded her knife and climbed onto the bed with the carcass.

***

The ringing of the doorbell interrupted Amy's work.

"Sheriff's department," said someone outside.

Amy climbed off the bed, feeling panic begin to rise in her breast. She calmed herself with the knowledge that she was now one of the chosen ones, written in the Book of Death. She had sworn the Oath of the Goat. Her master would keep her safe from all mortal authorities. Still, she had better take some simple precautions. She rushed into her mother's ensuite and cleaned the blood from her lips and teeth, then went into the living room as quietly as she could and began to conceal all evidence of criminal activity. She shoved her blood-splattered clothes into the laundry hamper beneath a clean towel and placed her folding knife into her back pocket. Meanwhile the bell rang again and again, and someone knocked heavily on the door.

"Sheriff's department," they said. "We can hear you in there. Please open up."

Amy answered the door and tried to act casual. She found herself facing two deputies, a male and a female. They had their hats in their hands and there was an odd, somber air about them. They introduced themselves by name and rank, then the female officer asked "May we come in, please? We have something to discuss."

"Sure," said Amy. She shrugged, but her heart was hammering.

They followed her into the living room.

"Please sit down," said the female officer.

Amy sat on the couch, and the female deputy sat beside her, while the male loitered on the periphery of the room in a way that made Amy even more nervous.

"Do you know a man named Tom Weegger?"

"Yeah, I know him," said Amy, while inside she thought *that sniveling worm, he's gone and told them everything! I should have killed him back at the house when I had the chance.*

"I'm sorry to have to tell you this," said the deputy, "but Tom died this morning. He killed himself. He left a note which mentions you. The original is evidence, but here is a copy."

The deputy handed Amy a grainy photocopy. As she glanced at it, she realized she'd never seen Tom's handwriting before. It was neat, almost girlish.

Amy, it's too late for me. I've gone to far. But you can still go back, you can still save yourself. Stay away from the Brimstone.

Amy folded the note and handed it back.

"Does the message mean much to you?"

asked the officer.

Amy shrugged. "Not really. To be honest we weren't that close, it was just a casual thing. I was about to break it off with him. He was into all this weird occult stuff." Amy shrugged, tried to look vaguely sad, then sat up and gestured to the front door. "I guess you can go now."

The deputy rose, then looked down at the couch. Following the woman's gaze, Amy saw a half-dozen Brimstone pills lying on the couch cushion. They must have slipped out of her pocket when she'd sat down and rolled into the space between the cushion and her thigh.

Fuck, she thought.

The male deputy echoed her thought out loud. "Fuck!" he shouted.

Amy turned to see him peeking into her mother's room, a horrified look spreading across his eyes as he beheld the mutilated corpse with its strips of missing flesh. His gun came out of his holster a moment later.

Amy reached for the knife in her back pocket. Before she could remove it something lanced into her breast. Paralyzing pain surged through her body as the female deputy deployed a 50,000 volt taser. Amy fell to the ground, her teeth locked in a rictus, as powerless as a puppet on a string.

***

Amy lay on the bottom bunk listening to a desperate inmate bashing a cell door somewhere down the block. Her cellmate snored above her like a wildebeest.

Amy adjusted the pillow under her head and closed her eyes. She didn't want to see them again. It was always around this time of night, in the smallest, darkest hours, that they came to her.

"Amy," came the familiar voice, high-pitched and childish. "Amy!"

Something compelled her to open her eyes. She saw them filing into the room, emerging from a shadow in the corner as though it were a doorway. Jimmy came first as always, flipping a black coin in his hand. He was naked, scalded, wet with blood-dimmed water.

The others came after - Will with his gruesome mutilations; the old man with his stab wounds; Tom with the noose around his neck; and finally Mom, a husk with black bile lips and strips of missing flesh. They all carried a coin each. Tom held his in his teeth, gnawing on it like a bit. There was one coin left. Jimmy held it out to her. It was black and covered in grave dirt, the same coin she had buried in the cemetery all those nights ago. Amy recoiled from it, but couldn't look away. She wanted to scream, but again something stopped her, some force that owned her, body and soul. She felt pinned in place like a frog on a dissection board.

Jimmy took her hand and shoved the filthy coin into her palm. The edges were sharp enough to cut through flesh.

"I don't want it," she muttered.

"But it's yours," he said. "You asked for it."

"I don't want it!"

"Tough luck. It's yours, and your time has come."

She whimpered. "No."

"But he wants you. You belong to him, and now you have to go to him."

"No," she whispered again.

The spirits cajoled her, like a chorus in an old Greek tragedy.

"Come on Amy, it's so easy. Let go. It's just like a dream."

"It's fun."

"It's easy."

"Just like a beautiful dream."

Amy managed to shriek "No!"

"Just do what you're told, you little bitch," said the old man.

"She was always a stubborn child," said Mom. "That's why her father ran off."

Amy curled up into a ball. Jimmy grabbed her. He still looked like a child, but he was so hideously strong. The others joined in, grasping her limbs, pulling at her body, until the razor-sharp coin was in her hand, and her hand was at her throat, pressing the deadly edge against the skin.

Amy felt hot arterial blood pulsing out onto her shoulder. As she bled out, her eyes widened and she caught a glimpse beyond the rotting veil of the world.

It wasn't at all what she'd expected to see.

FIN

SCARLET HOSANNA

Graves are best robbed by daylight.

The vampire's advice echoed in Hosea's head as he stood in the cemetery beneath the blazing sun. He wiped the sweat from his forehead and looked over his shoulder before wedging the beak of his crowbar between the rusted pieces of the mausoleum door. The whole thing groaned on its hinges as he applied steady pressure. At length something popped, and the warped door drifted open, giving way to cool darkness within.

Hosea's heart pounded with excitement. The door was open, and now he stood on the threshold between the land of the living and that of the dead. He said a silent farewell to the daylight, and entered the crypt's cold embrace.

Inside the crypt, Hosea's skin broke out in gooseflesh. He saw a crude altar built into the back wall, above it a wooden statue of a suffering Christ. Kneeling, he ran his fingers across the rough surface of the wooden trapdoor in the center of the floor. He knew the rusty lock stood no chance against his crowbar.

He crammed the tool between the stone slab and the trapdoor, and began to lever it open. As the door loosened he caught a glimpse of nought but darkness. The timber cracked around the lock, but didn't give way. Impatient, Hosea wrenched the bar with all his might. The lock broke and the trapdoor banged open, revealing a narrow staircase. Hosea stood over it, and thought about the bones waiting to be harvested.

***

With each step you take, you open another door. It's a process, one which takes time and sacrifice. It will be painful. You will conceive and give birth to another you. You will carve your new self out of your old self. This is the Dark Rebirth. Succumb to its call. It's all about predators and prey. In the realm of Eternal Night, you get to choose for yourself. Maybe for the first time ever.
From a post by livingdeadbabe69 on www.embracethenight.org

***

By the time Hosea returned to the land of the living, it was dark but still just as humid.

"Out robbing graves, huh?"

Surprised, Hosea turned to see a young woman emerging from the mouth of a smaller mausoleum opposite the one he had just left. She was dressed somewhat like him, with a black hoodie, black torn jeans, and black boots. He recognized her as a girl from St Martin's, the school he'd recently dropped out of, except she hadn't looked so goth then, more like a teeny bopper. Now her blonde hair and Barbie doll clothes had been traded for dyed-black hair, a nose stud, and a pentagram ring that flashed in the moonlight.

"Haven't seen you at school for a while," she said as she approached.

Hosea stared at her, resisting the sudden urge to run. Girls always terrified him. What was this one's name? Lisa? Linda?

"Don't remember me?" she said. "I'm Lana. You're Hosea, right?"

He nodded. Words crawled in his throat like crippled things, dying before they could be born. Suddenly he blurted "I'm turning into a vampire."

Lana's eyes, highlighted with thick black mascara, looked upon him with what seemed to be a deeper sense of appreciation. "Cool," she said.

Hosea couldn't hide his shock. That word - "cool" - was the last adjective he'd expected a girl to apply to him. "W-what?"

"Did you think I was expecting to find a normal person around here? What kind of guy hangs out in an old mausoleum? You came out of that crypt like some boogieman."

She smiled at him, and Hosea felt paralyzed. He'd never received such positive attention from a female who wasn't a close relative. A part of him wanted to respond in kind, but his fear overwhelmed him, and he found himself reacting with instinctive defensiveness. "It's none of your business," he said. "And you're not supposed to be here."

"Aspiring vampires only, huh?" she said.

"Something like that."

"Fine dude, whatever. I'm leaving now anyway."

"Good," Hosea said, even though a part of him desperately wanted her to stay.

He watched her turn and head towards the graveyard's western gate. Hosea was about to head in the opposite direction when he heard her call out to him.

"Tomorrow night, vampire?"

"Maybe," he replied.

"Alright. See ya."

She was gone before Hosea could respond.

***

Your Nexion is your safe haven. Build one. To build a temple is to reconstruct yourself anew. It is to create a physical space, a body, if you will, for the dark will to emanate forth. Before you can replace the spirit animating your flesh with an-

other, practice with a secluded space set apart from this world and dedicated to the night. Before you can harvest for your hunger, you should harvest for the Nexion. It will be a place of your own transgressions. A monument of your passage into the night; a vital cornerstone, a place of your own more than anything else in this world. There I will come to you. One way or the other. Sooner or later.

Post from Transilvanianprinceofdarkness666 on www.Lordsofthenight.org

***

Hosea awoke to the sound of voices. Sunlight shone through the dusty panes of his bedroom window. He could hear his parents talking in the kitchen. Their conversation was tense and muffled. Hosea caught only a single harsh phrase, spoken by his father -

"No son of mine's gonna turn out a faggot, Carla."

Hosea's mother began to say something in return but stopped abruptly. Her silence coincided with the sound of her being slapped across the face. Then the front door opened and closed with a slam that rattled the wooden skeleton they called a home. Out in the driveway, the car started, and

Hosea's father drove away.

Good, thought Hosea. It's better when he's gone.

Hosea got dressed as silently as possible, so as not to alert his mother to the fact he was awake. He didn't want to speak with her. As soon as he was ready he crept out the window and went on his way.

Out on the street he wasn't sure what to do. The cemetery was too busy with visitors on a Saturday; he wouldn't be able to go there till nightfall. Therefore the Nexion was the best possible place to spend the day.

As he headed to his haven, he thought about Lana. Would she really show up at the graveyard to meet him? A part of him desperately hoped so, despite the terror such a prospect made him feel.

As he crossed the humid woods he thought about his parents. Mom was probably still at home, crying. His dad was probably getting drunk somewhere. Hosea was tired of them both. Tired of them talking like they knew him. If they only knew the truth - he wouldn't be their son much longer, not after the Dark Rebirth.

A fallen tree lay against a rock. Hosea imagined the tree as a shackled female victim. He let out a feral cry and strode toward it.

Fucking die!

He picked up a thick stick and began beating the trunk.

Fucking die bitch, I'll fucking cut you up if you fucking scream.

He sank his teeth into the rotten wood and imagined biting into flesh.

Fucking stay quiet and I'll be gone soon and none of this ever happened or I'll fucking come and kill you. Just suck it up, little bitch, and let me finish.

***

Hosea,
It's been almost a week now. Your funeral's next Saturday. Not sure if I'll come. I'm sorry. Can't stop thinking about what happened. Did you really want to hurt me like this? Did you want to show me how you've been hurt? Was it an attack, or an invitation? I've been thinking we're like ghosts to one another. That's at least how I feel. Ghosts stop haunting when they are at peace, right? Is that what you wanted? To be my eternal boogeyman? Am I closer to you now than I ever was?
-Lana

***

Hosea emerged from the crypt to find Lana sitting at the base of a towering funerary monument, waiting for him. Cigarette butts lay scattered around her boots and pale ankles.

"So, a vampire?" she said.

"Yeah." Hosea stared at his muddy boots, avoiding eye contact, only daring to look directly at her when she herself glanced away. She had tied her hair back tonight, and her pale, delicate features looked beautiful in the wash of the moonlight.

"How do you become one?" she asked. "A vampire."

"I'm not sure…if I can tell you," he said. His cheeks felt hot. He couldn't believe she was actually here; girls usually avoided him like a plague.

"Bullshit," Lana laughed. "You're making it all up."

"No I'm not."

"Then tell me," she said.

"I send them emails," he said, surprised by his own talkativeness. Speaking to Lana was easier than he'd thought it would be.

"You email vampires?" she said. "Seriously?"

"Yeah. And there's this messageboard I found on the internet at school."

"But you don't go to school anymore."

"I got all the information I needed before I left. And there's a computer at the library I can use. I don't need school for anything, the place is useless."

"So you don't need school," she said. "But do you need blood?"

"It's...it's complicated," he said. "I don't need blood per se. Only a true vampire does. I'm still in the chrysalis stage. I haven't gone through the Blood Ritual, haven't experienced the Dark Rebirth. When I -"

Lana rolled her eyes. "I don't need the whole rulebook, just the CliffsNotes. Do you drink blood or not?"

"Of course I do," he snapped, even though he'd never tasted a drop. "What's it to you?"

"I asked," she said, "because I want you to drink from me." She didn't laugh; her tone lacked all previous suggestions of irony. "After all, a girl doesn't meet a vampire every night - not even an aspiring one. This might be my only chance to get sucked on by the real thing. So, do you want to feed on me, or what?"

Hosea nodded, even though he had no idea what to do next. He tongued one of his canines; it felt disappointingly blunt. He felt a mounting sense of performance anxiety, which threatened to overwhelm him, until Lana pulled a folded knife out of her pocket, opened it, and offered him its black plastic handle. He grasped it with a clammy hand.

Lana rolled up her sleeve, revealing a constellation of red wounds on white skin. Some were recent and scabbed over, like mouths filled with dirt; others had scarred over into the likeness of pink, bulging worms.

Lana looked him in the eye. Neither one of them said a word. She took his hand - the one holding the knife - and guided it toward her until the blade lay poised above an unblemished patch of skin near the crook of her arm. Hosea trembled; he didn't feel worthy.

"Do it," she said.

Hosea pressed the knife down. Lana's skin knelt before the steel. He stopped when she jerked back, fearing she had changed her mind. He released her arm and saw that he had marked the fair skin with a fresh, bleeding wound. Lana smiled and gestured for him to drink from it.

Hosea tasted the salty blood, and his heart thundered with an excitement he'd never known before.

After a while, Lana took her arm back, and said "You should email me too sometime, like you email those vampires." She went into her coffin-shaped backpack and produced a pen and paper. "Write your address here."

Hosea wrote down his email.

Lana eyed it dubiously. "Necromancer85@hotmail.com?"

Hosea shrugged. "Yours any better?"

Lana jotted her email down and ripped the page from the notebook.

Hosea read it out. "Darkbrokenbeauty@hotmail.com. Suits you."

Hosea had spoken without thinking. Self-consciousness rushed over him, making his face flush. He rose and hurried away before his embarrassment could get any worse.

"I've got to go," he said without looking back. "See you around."

"Back here again?" said Lana.

"Sure," he said, and fled into the maze of graves.

***

Hosea arrived home to find the light on in the carport. His dad sat in shadow just beyond the light, raising a cigarette to his lips. Hosea tried to swallow the rising panic in his throat. Maybe if he hurried past, Dad would leave him alone. He hurried through the cloud of cigarette smoke, offering a nod to acknowledge his father's presence. On the way past he spied the empty whisky bottle next to Dad's foot. He was almost at the house when his father said "Son."

Hosea stopped just outside the house.

"Come here."

Hosea turned and entered the faint ball of greasy light in the center of the carport.

"Closer."

Hosea did as he was told. His father's drunken gaze lurched up at him.

"Son, you gotta be able to take care of yourself." He sprang up with a pair of old boxing gloves dangling from his fist. "Put these on, and hit me."

Hosea shook his head.

"I said put these on, and hit me."

Hosea took a step back, silently refusing. Dad slapped him across the side of his head, leaving his ear ringing.

"Defend yourself!" spat the old man. "Stand up for yourself!"

Hosea's face grew hot. His father swung again before Hosea could move out of reach. This time a clenched fist slammed into his abdomen. Hosea doubled over in pain, winded, gasping for air.

"Straighten up!" Dad yelled. "Defend yourself. You're not a faggot. My son's not a goddamn queer!"

Dad took another swing. This one connected with Hosea's temple. For a second the world went black, but Hosea regained his senses before he hit the ground. He stumbled back in a rush of pain and disorientation. This wasn't the first time he'd taken a beating from Dad, but something was different this time. The old man seemed wild, murderous even. For the first time Hosea noticed the drops of blood on his father's clothing. A terrible thought gripped his mind.

Mom.

Hosea turned and headed for the house. He was still groggy from the headstrike, and the ground seemed to sway beneath his feet, as though he were on the deck of a boat at sea. He found the front door open and floated into the darkness beyond. Inside, the familiar labyrinth of his family home was unnaturally still.

"Mom?" he called out, just before he found her lying on the floor, blood pooled around her head like a halo. She was motionless, breathless. Looking down at her, Hosea felt strangely detached, as if he were watching the whole scene happen to someone else.

"Goodbye Mom," said Hosea. "You should have never tried to save me."

A moment later, Dad staggered into the kitchen and knelt beside Mom. With tears in his eyes he brushed bloody hair from her face.

Urged by instinct, Hosea fled from the house and into the woods.

***

Dark knowledge can be distilled from every experience. One systematic way is to go to the extremes of one's own experience and turn that experience around. For example, a victim of abuse knows the very real foundations for violent dominance. All he must do is use his will and put that knowledge into use. Aim the knife back from whence it came. Own the abuse from the inside out.

If one seeks to attain a full, imperishable inhuman center of being, no other options remain than seeking the utmost borders of annihilation, depravity, and moral decoding.

Watch videos of beheadings and school shootings. Look for the most extreme art, transforming the sensible world order with raw, unfiltered emotion. Scavenge graves to experience the most disgusting, inhuman odors, tastes, and visual depravity. Own it all. Own yourself, your life, and learn to own your death. See the world like flies and worms do. Roam it like a jackal.

You'll begin to understand the dark order

beneath all things.

It is not the doctrine that is important. It is the meaning you breathe into it. The way you embody it. There is no evil in a world void of false hope, in an existence lacking human-centrism.

The necessities of obedience and peace are young inventions. Our complex bodies and selves, having been forged in the unwritten darkness of the past millenniums, are alien to them. The requirement of humane tameness is but an illusion at the eye of a storm so profound we've yet to comprehend it.

From a post by Countessbathorysdemonlover on www.lordsofthenight.org

***

Lana woke to the sound of her bedroom door opening, and looked up from her pillow to see her little sister Andrea approaching. The child looked spooked, as though she'd awoken from a nightmare. "Can I sleep with you?" she asked.

"Sure," said Lana, shuffling over to make space in the bed.

Andrea climbed in, and Lana pulled the blanket over both of them. As Lana settled back into a comfortable position, Andrea remained tense, peeking anxiously over the edge of the quilt.

Lana stroked her sister's blonde curls. "What's the matter? Scared of monsters in the basement again? It's just an ordinary basement. Besides, it's all the way downstairs."

"I'm not scared of the basement," said Andrea. "I saw him at my window."

Lana felt her body tense up. "Saw who?"

"I couldn't see properly. I was too scared."

Lana climbed out of bed and went to her window. Drawing back the curtain, she saw a series of dark smudges on the outside of the glass resembling runes from some primitive, pagan alphabet. Lana leaned closer and saw the markings had been made with blood; she could just make out whorls and loops of fingerprints in the fresh-looking smears. She smiled to herself and turned to Andrea.

"Is there a monster?" asked Andrea.

Lana closed the curtain on the bloodstains. "No, there's nothing there. Let's go to sleep."

Lana climbed back into bed and kissed Andrea goodnight. Soon the child was asleep, while Lana remained awake, peering through the crack of the curtain at a sliver of night. The crimson rune was hidden from sight, but clear in her mind.

***

Lana woke up alone. She raised her head from her pillow and heard Andrea talking with Mom in the kitchen downstairs.

Lana walked to the bathroom across the hall. She pulled a wad of toilet paper from the roll and soaked it under warm water. Back in her room, she opened her window and washed the bloody markings away before anyone else could see them. She knew they were meant only for her, from her special vampire. He must have gone to Andrea's room first, by accident, she thought. If only he'd found her room right off the bat, she could have let him in.

From now on, she decided, she'd sleep naked with her window open and her door locked. If Andrea wanted comfort in the night, she could go see Mom and Dad instead. Lana didn't want to miss out on the next visit from Hosea. Scenarios of passion ripped from sexy vampire movies ran vividly through her mind.

Lana covered the marks of her cutting with long sleeves and pants, as she always did, then went downstairs to where a cup of coffee and pancakes waited on the kitchen counter. Mom bustled around, scraping leftovers into the trash. Andrea sat engrossed in the act of drawing with her pencils; she probably didn't even remember her scare from the night before.

"Hey, honey," said Mom. "Your sister and I were thinking of going out of town for a bit. You wanna come?"

"For how long?" asked Lana, pretending to be open to the idea.

"Overnight, at least. Visit Aunt Doris, do a little shopping. Interested?"

"I'd rather stay here."

"Well, you are seventeen, so I suppose I can't force you. But just think of all the fun you'll be missing!"

"I think I'll keep the house warm. Thanks."

Mom rolled her eyes. "Teenagers," she said. "Alright. We'll pack and go. Dad's already left on his big business trip. You'll be home all alone. Don't go throwing any parties. And be safe, okay?"

"I'll be alright, Mom. I swear."

"I know, I know. But I'm your Mom, I'm supposed to worry, at least a little bit." She turned to Andrea. "Okay, sweetie pie, pack up your pencils, we've gotta get ready."

Lana smiled to herself. A few days alone didn't bother her - but it was the nights she was really looking forward to.

***

Hosea,

I know I never said it to you, but I've always left my window open for you. Still do. Sad it's getting cold. Our summer's gone. Wish you would have told me. I really wanted to be your friend.

-Lana

***

Hosea sat cross-legged in the basement of the abandoned house which served as his Nexion. The altar he had painstakingly constructed stood before him, a skull atop a pile of stray bones bound by barbed wire. He ran his finger across the fur of a dead rat that lay between him and the altar. It was stiff and wet. He probed a large wound on its stomach.

"Do you like to play with dead things?"

"I suppose," said Hosea, not daring to look up in the direction of the voice. "Are you really here? Are you really...real?"

"As real as your Mom."

In his mind's eye, Hosea saw his Mom lying face down in a mirror-like pool of black blood on the kitchen floor. A pale arm emerged from the pool as if from a doorway, and clawed at Mom's scalp with black talons.

Hosea opened his eyes and found himself staring into the empty sockets of the altar skull.

He wondered, not for the first time, but with an as-yet unknown sense of clarity, what it would be like to exist in a state of undeath - to dwell on the inverse side of being, not a living thing but a metaphysical entity, a scar carved into the tissue of time and space, free of fear, free of guilt - free even from the dubious dignity and undeniable torment of human agency.

Despite his fear, Hosea couldn't wait.

He stood up and went to the door - more of a hole, really - which led from his Nexion into the forest. He emerged into the calm of the woods. It was night. Time to head for the cemetery. He was eager for his rendezvous with Lana. A part of himself he despised as weak simply craved her presence, while the other part - the dark inner self to which he was giving birth - yearned to taste her blood again. Every drop was like another red brick on the path to his ascension.

***

Hosea reached the summit of the forested hill just outside the cemetery. The hidden space was wild with thickets and allowed him to survey the surrounding area without being noticed. He took in the sprawling cemetery down below. It was still and quiet, just how he liked it.

Not far beyond the graveyard, Hosea's former school complex broke up the landscape with its scattering of sodium lights and stark chain link borders. Remembering the cruel, ugly faces of his "peers" made him feel sick. *Fuck them,* he thought, knowing that when he made his return they'd regret every insult and injury they'd ever dared to inflict upon him. He took comfort in the idea that someday soon the cemetery was going to gain a few extra souls, the more the better. The idea made him eager to be on his way. He was tired of planning, of waiting; the time for action was swiftly approaching.

He descended the hill and easily scaled the cemetery's crumbling brick wall. As he headed through the graves toward his and Lana's meeting place, he made a mental checklist of what he'd need from home in order to prepare for his final act of ascension. His duffle bag was filled with his notes from the vampire forums and the emails he'd received, plus a how-to guide for constructing explosives. The bag would be easy to get; he remembered exactly where he'd left it. The thing he needed the most, Dad's rifle, might be trickier to obtain, depending on how things had gone down after he'd run off last night. Had his dad called the police? Probably not. Shot himself? Maybe. Just kept drinking? Most likely. Whatever the case, Hosea had no intention of sticking around very long when he returned. He'd be in and out quick with his supplies, then onward to his final act as a pitiful human. All his weakness would perish in flames. His soul would be baptized in death. His flesh -

"Hey vampire."

Lana's voice derailed his train of thought and almost made him jump. She'd emerged from a clump of shadowed monuments behind him, and stood in the humid moonlight, wearing a short black dress. Her presence paralyzed him with shyness, just another sign of the humanity he longed to be rid of. Nevertheless he wanted to be near her.

"You never emailed me," she said. "But I got your message."

Before he could ask what message she was talking about, Lana drew closer, so close he could smell her hair and perfume, so close he felt he could even feel the heat coming off her body to mingle with the warmth of the night. Her bare arms and legs shone in the moonlight. He saw once again the constellations of scars on her arms, but he also saw for the first time the scars on her thighs, clustered so close together they looked like wrinkles on pale wrapping paper someone had scrunched up and then carefully folded flat. The scars were clustered on her inner thighs, just below her sex. Just inches from his clammy hand. An electric tingle ran through him, part excitement, part fear. An instinct of shyness so deep it lay in his bones told him to flee back to his Nexion, but he forced himself to remain, even when she stepped so close their skin was almost touching.

"I'm sorry you weren't able to come in last night," she said. "Next time, I'll make sure Andrea isn't there. Then we can be alone, just like we are now."

Hosea had no idea who or what she was talking about. Was she roleplaying? The frenzy of his nerves made it hard for him to concentrate, hard to ask meaningful questions. His skin felt hot. His pulse was pounding. She stepped even closer, until her arm was touching his. Now he really could feel her warmth. Instinctive fear drove him to take a step back.

"Can I just drink?" he said. "At least for now?"

Lana acted as if she were thinking it over. "Sure," she said.

She rolled her sleeve up and pulled out her pocket knife. Hosea took the blade but paused before pressing it against her skin. His gaze was drawn to the wound he'd made the night before, still wrapped in a bandage; he could just make out the seepage of blood through the fabric. Everything about the wound - the fact he had made it, licked it, kissed it, drank from it - filled him with a sense of intimacy unlike anything he'd known before.

"Does it hurt?" he asked.

"Of course it hurts. Life does." She lit a cigarette and inhaled. "Hurt me again."

He pressed the blade into her skin and pulled it sideways. Lana made an involuntary grimace as blood welled into the small, narrow trench. Hosea licked and sucked at the wound. Again he felt that unparalleled sense of intimacy, as though she and he were becoming one flesh. He drank and drank, in a trance of delight, until she pulled her arm away.

"I think you've had enough," she said. "But don't worry, there's other parts of me you can taste."

She stepped close as if to kiss him. Once again, instinctive fear drove Hosea back. Lana peered at him, perplexed.

"Don't tell me you just want to drink my blood," she said.

Hosea stared at her, speechless with nerves.

"Are you serious?" she said.

Her laugh mingled rage with his fear. His face felt as if it were burning. Some deep part of him felt as if it were under attack. Suddenly he blurted out - "I'm not gay!"

"What?" said Lana.

Hosea couldn't answer. He turned and rushed away.

"Hey," she said, "wait, I never said anything! I never said you were - where are you going? Stop!"

But Hosea couldn't stop, even though a part of him wanted to remain with her so badly he felt as if steel hooks were pulling at his chest as he rushed off into the night. As he headed back to his Nexion, he could only comfort himself with the thought that his agonizing humanity would soon be gone forever.

***

That night Lana lay naked and alone in her room. She looked through her window, hoping for her vampire, but saw only the moon. She cut her finger with a razor and ran the wounded digit along the base of her neck and down between her breasts, marking her skin with blood, as if it might somehow draw him to her.

Lana's eyes teared up as her wound pulsed and shed wasted blood. She stared into the empty yard below. Tired of waiting, she smeared blood on her lips like gloss and kissed the windowpane, leaving a message of longing for the one she desired, and a red goodnight kiss to the darkness outside.

She left the window open and lay down to sleep. The blood dried on her skin. Thoughts of Hosea haunted her, but she didn't want it any other way.

***

Hosea found the front door hanging open. He peered inside, looking for movement but seeing none. He wondered if he'd find his father passed out in a puddle of vomit, maybe beside Mom's corpse. In any case he would avoid them both and head straight for what he needed, starting with his duffel bag.

He crept into the house. Mom's body was gone from where he'd found it earlier, but reminders of the woman were everywhere - on side tables, on the walls, in the furnishings and decor she'd chosen. Not even the darkness of the house could hide all the signs of her presence, so that she lingered after death, like a stubborn ghost.

Hosea pushed away the memories the house invoked, and stuck to the task at hand. Keeping to the shadows, he mounted the stairs and headed for his room. Dad was nowhere to be seen either; perhaps he was burying Mom at that very moment in some shallow woodland grave.

Hosea discarded the thoughts and entered his room. He pulled his duffel bag from under his bed and slung it over his shoulder. An anxious instinct told him to inspect the pack, to make sure everything was there, but the weight felt right, and he just wanted to get the hell out of the house. He began to leave the room, but froze as he caught sight of movement in the hall. A shadow slipped past the door, as fast as a beat of ravens' wings, and was gone. Downstairs a door slammed.

Hosea's heart beat faster. He crept into the hall and looked down the stairs; the front door was closed. It was only the wind, he told himself.

He crept down the stairs. The house was eerily silent. He stopped at the bottom of the stairs and peered around the living room. The lights were off. Through the front windows and the rustling branches of the trees outside fell a blanket of fitful moonlight, just enough to illuminate a series of dark stains on the couch. Blood, thought Hosea. More dark patches - these ones glistening on the timber floor - formed a trail leading straight to his parents' room, where Dad's gun lay concealed beneath the bed.

Hosea needed that gun, but a sudden sense of terror held him at bay. The air felt as though it were filled with electric dread, something uncanny. He stared across the living room into his parents' bedroom, where the trail of blood led into a zone of fuzzy darkness. He struggled to make out anything within. He forced himself to creep closer, avoiding the patches of blood on the floor, until he stood in the doorway looking in. Slowly the shapes inside began to materialize from the dark. He caught glimpses of blood splatter, torn throats, pale flesh butchered in feeble moonlight.

An arm slipped around Hosea's throat from behind so fast he didn't even have time to scream. The limb was unbelievably strong and as cold as dead, refrigerated meat. The pressure on his neck choked off his breath, his voice, the steady pulse of blood to his brain. Sheer terror flooded his system. He struggled but couldn't pull free. Another arm slipped around his waist, pulling him closer to the cold thing behind him. Hosea caught a whiff of its sour stench.

"Don't struggle, or you'll go to sleep and never wake up."

It was the same voice Hosea had heard in the Nexion. He had no choice but to obey. He grew still, and the pressure on his throat slackened, allowing him to breathe, allowing the blood to pump freely to his head. He heard it thunder in his ears as the thing spoke again.

"Look closely," it said. "See the truth of what I am, of what you would become."

Hosea peered into the room. The whole bed was black with blood. His parents lay there, reduced to a mangled pile of limbs pocked with deep puncture wounds. Only their eyes remained intact. Glistening, they seemed to stare at him with lidless intensity as his pants were ripped down from his waist, exposing his naked lower body.

"Don't resist," said the thing from the Nexion.

Hosea obediently dropped down on all fours. Cold hands grabbed his hips.

"I'll lead you through the vortex of death," said the thing. "Your dark rebirth will shake the world."

Images and memories flickered through Hosea's mind as if summoned by the thing behind him. Faces of people at school. Their glares, their mocking laughter. The tortures he'd endured. He thought about Dad's gun.

"We'll bathe in their blood together," promised the thing.

Hosea almost smiled, but then the painful violation began.

***

Lana woke up alone. The ghost of early morning lingered in her room. She stared at her dim surroundings and remembered her scarlet rite from the previous evening. She thought of Hosea, and felt a sense of apprehension she couldn't quite account for.

She went to her dad's office and switched on his computer, pacing while she waited for it to start up. She couldn't shake the eerie feeling that something bad had happened, and that Hosea was part of it.

As soon as the computer was ready she logged into her email, hoping to see a message from Hosea. There was nothing. She pressed refresh. Still nothing.

"Fuck."

She typed a hurried message, then turned off the computer and went back to her room. A ray of light shone through the window. With a shock, Lana realized the pane of glass was immaculately clean. She rushed over to it, searching for any trace of her own dried blood. There was nothing there, nothing but semi-transparent smears of saliva, left by whoever had licked the glass clean.

He visited me, she thought. He visited, but didn't wake me.

What did it mean? Was this a rejection, or another step in their strange courtship? Lana burned with frustration and obsession, with mingled anger and longing. She needed to know the truth of where she stood with this boy. She would return to the cemetery at once, and wait until he arrived, even if she had to wait all day and night among the dead.

***

Hosea entered the library, heavy with purpose and the weight of the duffel bag slung across his shoulders. He passed through mostly vacant aisles of books. Whispers and muffled bursts of laughter drifted from the occupied corners of the building, where students crowded around, socializing under the pretext of studying. The thought of them filled him with a cold rage, but he moved on, making his way towards the public computers. A small blonde girl stood in the aisle, blocking his path. He glared at her, and she ran off, vanishing amongst the tall shelves and leaving the way clear.

He set his duffel down and sat in front of one of several unoccupied computer desks. This would only take a moment. He had only one message to send - perhaps the most important message of his life. Then he would continue on to the school, on to the ritual of his Dark Rebirth.

He logged in and saw an email from Lana.

I'm sorry about what happened. I just for some reason thought that that was what you wanted too. Sorry I mistook you. Didn't mean to. Just wanted to say I'm sorry. Gonna be at our place hanging out until you get there. When you feel like it, come. Please. It'll be alright, okay?

-Lana

Hosea finished reading, and breathed a sigh of relief. He was glad she'd be safe at the cemetery, away from the school. He wanted so much to answer her in detail - to pour out his soul and tell her absolutely everything - but he only had time for a quick response.

Lana,

Not sure if I'm really becoming a vampire. If not, it's alright... Then I'll just be ordinary-gone. The way I kinda always wanted. But just in case... If some morning you happen to see a bloody print left on your window... It could be mine.

-Hosea

PS: Apology accepted.

***

Lana entered the cemetery and made her way directly to their special meeting place. The same mix of frustration and obsession continued to torment her. She rehearsed infuriated litanies, practicing how she would condemn him for flaking out on her, for toying with her feelings, for hovering around her window without daring to enter. She practiced spiteful tirades, how she'd curse him as a weakling, as a queer. But the anger left her hollow with sadness, and she couldn't stay mad at him. Of all the people in this dead-end town, he was the only one like her. The only one who knew the beautiful darkness beyond the mainstream, the glorious abysses that lurked beyond white picket fences, the secret beauty of monstrosity and otherness. When all was said and done, she just wanted him to come to her, no matter what. She wouldn't even care if he never even kissed her, never even touched her. Even if all he could do was watch her from a distance, that alone would be enough, as long as she could be sure of his presence, his closeness, his equal and insatiable longing.

She peered around the graves, hoping to see him striding toward her, but she was alone with the dead. Moved by a nameless instinct, Lana took out her blade and sliced into her index finger. With the dripping digit she drew a heart on the wall of the mausoleum where first they had met. She stared at the drying redness, thinking of what might still come to be, until the wailing of sirens broke through her daydreams. She turned to see a vast convoy of emergency vehicles flying past the graveyard - police, ambulance, fire brigade, all of them on their way to St Martin's high school. The various sirens combined into a dissonant, apocalyptic symphony.

Something big was going down.

***

Violence gives birth to nightmares, and violence ends them. It is an eternal dance, as long as there is a man witnessing it. Make your choice. You've never had one before. Probably never will again.

From a post by Carpathianoverlord666, on www.vampiresovmidianunite.org, 12/05/1999

***

Smoke poured through the school's hallways. Hosea's firebombs had all detonated, setting most of the eastern wing ablaze. A demonic symphony of fire alarms and screams filled the building. Panicked figures moved through the smoke. Hosea took aim with his father's assault rifle and fired towards them. Some fled on, whilst others fell to the ground, their sounds of panic truncated by the boom of the rifle.

Hosea walked on through the smoke and pandemonium. He thrilled to the knowledge that he had made the school become for others what it had always been for him - Hell on Earth.

He stopped at what had been the Ninth Circle of Hell - his old biology class. He tried the handle, and found the door locked. Smoke thickened around him, accumulating in his throat, choking him. He had to keep moving if he wanted to live, but he couldn't give up this chance for revenge. He took a step back and fired through the door, unloading most of the clip. Wood chips flew from the brutal holes the bullets created. Screams and cries of agony erupted from the room beyond, but Hosea could barely hear them over the ringing in his ears. The repeated gunfire had dampened his hearing into a murky haze of tinnitus.

He kicked the door open. The corpse of his most hated teacher, Mr Henderson, lay half-obliterated on the floor. Other corpses lay strewn nearby. The rest of the survivors were bunched up at the back of the room, like cattle trapped in a pen, trying to flee despite the absence of any real exit. There were more familiar faces in the crowd - Jenny Carmichael, who'd called him a try-hard goth and a chicken-fucker; Eric Dupont, who'd given him a wedgie and called him a pole smoker; and Peter Kincaid, who'd held him down and hocked loogies into his mouth one day in the parking lot after school.

Hosea turned the rifle on them all and held the trigger till the clip was almost empty and the back of the room was a mound of wet death. He wanted to keep firing - to reduce the little that remained of those bodies to pulp - but he feared using up all of the bullets. He needed to save at least one.

The smoke thickened, and Hosea coughed again. It was growing almost impossible to breathe, almost impossible to see. The heat from approaching fires grew heavier, more oppressive. He knew there was not much more time to complete his ritual, to ensure his Dark Rebirth.

He ran his hand across the splintered remains of the door. His palm was slashed to ribbons in the process, but for the first time in his life he felt no pain. He wiped his blood on the nearby wall, then used his finger to write a three-digit number in the center of the smear, creating a ragged 666.

He coughed. Smoke blinded his eyes. He could feel his skin begin to blister from the rising heat. He knew this was it, this was the moment. The ritual had to be completed now, or it would all be too late.

Hosea sank to his knees, stuck the barrel of

the rifle in his mouth, and pulled the trigger. In his final moment, he wished that Lana were with him.

***

Hosea,

Sorry I keep writing to you. It's pretty dumb to write to a dead guy. It's just... I don't have anyone else, you know? It's horrible to have to pretend I was lucky not to be there. On most days I wish I could have left with you. I've been a mess, to be honest. It's been a whole summer. School starts again next week. The paper ran a story about it again. It had their photos in it. The article talked about the new term that was starting. How it was time to come together again and heal. There was not a single mention of you. I'm just mad about it. It hurts too much. Mad about what you did. Mad that you never told me how to be with you. Mad that you never entered my room. There are days I just wanna stop writing to you completely. Sometimes I wish you never existed at all. Then there are days I'm just so sorry I even had such a thought. I suppose today's the latter.

666,

-Lana

***

Lana woke up to find Andrea sobbing beside her bed. The little girl looked terrified.

"What's up, sis?" said Lana, still groggy from sleep.

"The monster's back." Andrea trembled. The look of sheer dread in her eyes made Lana wonder if this was more than just a case of a child's overactive imagination. Feeling suddenly and vividly awake, Lana got up and gestured for Andrea to take her place under the sheets.

"You hop in here and wait while I go check it out," she said.

Reluctantly, Andrea climbed under the covers and hid there.

Lana crept into the hallway. An unseasonal draft caressed her bare ankles. She passed her father's office and drew closer to Andrea's room. On the way the breeze grew colder, carrying a bitter aroma of smoke.

She reached her sister's room to find the window open, the white curtain fluttering. Lana rushed over and closed it. The breeze died and stillness filled the room, but somehow the bitter smell of smoke grew stronger, as though it were trapped with her. She noticed smears on the pane and the windowsill, dark and acrid-smelling, like wet ashes.

Lana peered into the gloom outside. "Hosea?" she whispered.

"Unfortunately, no."

The voice came from behind her.

"Who are you?" asked Lana, unable to turn around and face the speaker, held in place by a preternatural fear unlike any she'd ever felt before.

"I'm the one you called with your blood, the one you wanted. But I'm probably not what you imagined."

Lana's breath stalled in her throat. She still couldn't move, could barely breathe. Her bladder emptied of its own accord.

"I am going downstairs now," said the monster. "I'll rip your parents apart, then your sister."

"Why?"

"Why not? Besides, I'm just entering where I've been invited."

There was no sound of movement, but the acrid smell lifted, and Lana knew she was alone again in the room. Nevertheless she remained paralyzed, even when the screaming started.

FIN

About the Author

Henry Ben Edom is a Finnish horror author, cat dad, and a life-long lover of the macabre. His short fiction has previously been published in anthologies by imprints such as Eerie River Publishing, TK Pulp, and Hellbound Books. He can be usually found somewhere dark and underground.

Other Books From

Where The Worm Never Dies
by Quinn Hernandez

Dog Men
by Gavin Torvik

Doomsday Daytrip
by Rob Ramirez

Cigarette Lemonade
by Connor de Bruler

Temperance Holocaust
by BJ Swann
and Elizabeth Bedlam

**FOR MORE BOOKS CHECK OUT
SWANNBEDLAM.COM**

**FOLLOW US ON INSTAGRAM
@SWANN.BEDLAM**

**BECOME AN ARC READER EMAIL US AT
SWANNANDBEDLAM@GMAIL.COM**

Milton Keynes UK
Ingram Content Group UK Ltd.
UKHW040115120624
443985UK00004B/87

9 780645 958676